Ethiopian Music

MICHAEL POWNE

Ethiopian Music

AN INTRODUCTION

A SURVEY OF ECCLESIASTICAL
AND SECULAR ETHIOPIAN MUSIC
AND INSTRUMENTS

GREENWOOD PRESS, PUBLISHERS
WESTPORT, CONNECTICUT

Library of Congress Cataloging in Publication Data

Powne, Michael.
    Ethiopian music.

    Reprint of the ed. published by Oxford University
Press, London, New York.
    Bibliography: p.
    Includes index.
    1. Music, Ethiopic--History and criticism.
2. Musical instruments, Ethiopic. 3. Musical
instruments, Primitive. I. Title.
[ML3760.P69 1980]   781.763   80-14087
ISBN 0-313-22161-8 (lib. bdg.)

For E. M. L. P.

781.763
P889

This reprint has been authorized by the Oxford University
Press.

Reprinted in 1980 by Greenwood Press,
a division of Congressional Information Service, Inc.
88 Post Road West, Westport, Connecticut 06881

Printed in the United States of America

10 9 8 7 6 5 4 3 2 1

Preface

This book sets out to present a conspectus of information about Ethiopian music. It falls naturally into three main sections:

I. Musical instruments.
II. Secular music.
III. Ecclesiastical music.

Except in the concluding remarks, no reference is made to the debased or westernized music that dominates the musical scene today in Ethiopia, as in most of Africa. I am concerned only with traditional music, its origins and growth, how it appears to have been performed in the past, and its performance today. The work is further limited in that it refers almost entirely to the music of the Hamo-Semitic plateaux peoples, making only cursory reference to other regions of the country. No serious comparison is made between Ethiopian music and the music of other cultures, nor does the book seek to show conclusively any connections there may be with other cultures. In the first chapter, however, I have tried to place the country and people in their proper context with regard to their history, geography, and ethnography. Without this information the effectiveness of an assessment of a people's music would be reduced. Its provision helps to illuminate the multitude of topics for

[v]

further study that are suggested by this book and the research that preceded it.

Much of the material was gathered in Addis Ababa, the capital of Ethiopia, between 1954 and 1960 and during a return visit in September 1963. Tape recordings were made of the National Folklore Orchestra of the Haile Selassie I Theatre and in Holy Trinity Cathedral. Further recordings were taken when the orchestra gave a series of folklore concerts in the National Theatre, Kampala, Uganda. The Museum of the Institute of Ethiopian Studies at Haile Selassie I University, Addis Ababa, was a valuable source of information about musical instruments ; and its Curator, Dr. Stanislaw Chojnacki, gave great help. Without doubt much important material exists in the Institute's library, as also in the National Library of Ethiopia, but these collections were at the time of writing still largely unclassified and little use could be made of them. A good deal of general information was found in the Africana section of the library of Makerere University College, Kampala.

Other largely untouched sources available to the student of Ethiopian music are the great collections of manuscripts[1] in Europe, especially in the British Museum, and the collection of instruments at the Horniman Museum, London. Of original writings on the subject there is a notable dearth.

Ethiopian music and hymnography still await examination and study. Apart from a few preliminary treatises and some pieces of scattered and often inaccessible information, the entire field is virgin soil. It is unlikely that one person alone will be sufficiently competent to tackle so complex an investigation; it would, therefore, be desirable to bring together a small team of experts to engage in thorough research into the history of Ethiopian music and its contemporary manifestations. . . . Much of the material may have to be gathered in Ethiopia, but the musical notation of the *Deggwa* can be studied in Europe, where some excellent MSS. of this work exist. It will also be possible to

---

[1] See p. 108, footnote 2.

work with Ethiopian informants temporarily in Europe and especially with the students of the Collegio Etiopico in the Vatican.[1]

Under 'Ethiopian Church Music', the *Harvard Dictionary of Music* (1951 edition) gives only five references, detailed fully in the Bibliography (page 149). The 1954 edition of *Grove* gives even fewer references. The most detailed list of articles is given by Ullendorff[2], including works in Italian, Arabic, Amharic, French, German, Latin, and English. The earliest are Marianus Victorius' grammar of Ge'ez (the language of the Orthodox Church of Ethiopia), which has a brief appendix 'De Musica Aethiopium' and was published in 1552, and H. Ludolf's *Commentarius ad suam Historiam Aethiopicam* (Frankfurt, 1691), which has brief references. Ullendorff attaches considerable importance to 'the first competent study of Oriental music', by Villoteau,[3] and to 'the most detailed account of Ethiopian music hitherto published', by C. Mondon-Vidailhet.[4] An article by Egon Wellesz[5] is of great value. I am grateful to Mlle. Simone Wallon[6] for drawing attention to two further articles of substance.[7] The only lengthy study in English is to be found in Sylvia Pankhurst's ponderous *Ethiopia: A Cultural History* (London, 1955). The great majority of all these works deal with the music of the Church, and it is only Mondon-Vidailhet and Pankhurst who have anything of real value on secular music.

This book draws quite heavily upon the work of Mondon-Vidailhet and Pankhurst, as well as on other authorities in

---

[1] *The Ethiopians* by E. Ullendorff (2nd ed., London, 1965), p. 169.
[2] ibid. pp. 170–1.
[3] *Description de l'Egypte* (Paris, 1799).
[4] 'La musique éthiopienne', *Encyclopédie de la musique et dictionnaire du Conservatoire*, 1st part (Paris, 1922).
[5] 'Studien zur aethiopischen Kirchenmusik', *Oriens Christianus*, 1920.
[6] Librarian, Music Dept., Bibliothèque Nationale, Paris.
[7] G. Barblan, *Musiche e strumenti musicali nell' Africa orientale italiana* (Naples, 1941); H. Hickmann, 'Aethiopische Musik', *Die Musik in Geschichte und Gegenwart* (Kassel, 1949/51).

lesser degree. However, considerably more than half of its material is original in that it was collected first-hand in Ethiopia. No guarantee can be offered as to its accuracy in all respects, as a good deal of the information gathered there conflicted with the findings of Mondon-Vidailhet and Pankhurst; and, indeed, individual knowledgeable Ethiopians contradicted one another on a number of points. One of the difficulties in the work was that there is no Ethiopian who may be quoted as an undisputed authority on any musical topic, except perhaps that of the interpretation of the liturgical notation system.

Two further instances may be quoted to show how great is the scarcity of knowledge of Ethiopia and its music. A. M. Jones has published[1] a map of Africa showing the distribution patterns of typical harmonic usages in the continent. This shows which tribes and areas use predominantly 4th, 3rds, etc., in their harmonizations. Ethiopia is conspicuous by being a large blank space : the only blank space on the map. Hugh Tracey[2] told me in 1961 that of his 14,000 separate tape-recorded items of African music not one came from Ethiopia ; but he had recordings from nearly every other corner of Africa.

M. P.

Bath, 1965

NOTE:

There are two main sources for the original research embodied in this book. They are referred to in the text by the following abbreviated forms:

Museum—the Museum of the Institute of Ethiopian Studies, Haile Selassie I University, Addis Ababa.
Orchestra—the National Folklore Orchestra of the Haile Selassie I Theatre, Addis Ababa.

---

[1] *Studies in African Music* (London, 1959), p. 230.
[2] Director of the International Library of African Music, Roodepoort, Transvaal, S. Africa.

Contents

[ix]

List of Plates

Plates 2 and 5–10, taken in the Museum of the Institute of Ethiopian Studies, Haile Selassie I University, Addis Ababa, are reproduced by kind permission of the Director of the Institute, Plate 3 by kind permission of Hanns Reich Verlag, München (reproduced from *Aethiopien*), Plate 4 by kind permission of the Curator of the Horniman Museum. Plates 1 and 11 were taken at Holy Trinity Cathedral, Addis Ababa, by Roger Barnes. Figures 1, 2, 4, and 5 are reproduced from *Ältvölker Süd-Äthiopien* by kind permission of W. Köhlhammer, Frankfurt-am-Main.

[xi]

Acknowledgements

I wish to express my warmest appreciation of the help given by the people named here. I have benefited from their assistance, advice or knowledge in countless different ways; without this I could not have gathered the material for the book, or worked it into shape.

1. *At Haile Selassie I University, Addis Ababa*
   in the Library: Mrs. R. Pankhurst; in the Institute of Ethiopian Studies: Dr. R. Pankhurst, Dr. S. Chojnacki, and Mr. S. Wright; in the Creative Arts Centre: Dr. P. Caplan, Dr. Halim El-Dabh, and Mr. Tesfaye Gessesse. Mr. Wright and Dr. El-Dabh receive special thanks for the great amount of time they spent in discussion with me.

2. *At the Haile Selassie I Theatre, Addis Ababa*
   Mr. Kebede Asfaw, Vice-Minister in charge, who gave me the fullest facilities for recording and studying.
   Mr. Tsegaye Gabre Medhin, Cultural Director, who gave much valuable information.
   Mr. Lakew Abebe, Mr. Lemma Gabre Hiwot, and all other members of the folklore orchestra, and the singing and dancing company.

3. *At Holy Trinity Cathedral, Addis Ababa*
   Like Siltanat Habte Mariam Workineh, Dean of the Cathedral, who provided me with every assistance and facility asked for.
   Kagn Geta Mesfin Hailemariam, Mr. Girma Wolde-kirkos and Mr. Aymro Mandefro, of the Theological College, who demonstrated the church singing to me.

4. Mr. Abebe Kebede, formerly Cultural Attaché at the Ethiopian Embassy in London, now Administrator-General of the Haile Selassie Foundation, who smoothed many paths for me.

Mr. Seyum Sebhat, formerly Cultural Director at the Haile Selassie Theatre, and his wife Alem Tsehai Asfaw, for much help with recordings.

The British Council, Addis Ababa, for loan of some tape recordings.

Mr. Peter Carpenter, Director of the National Theatre, Kampala, Uganda, for help with recordings.

Mr. Roger Barnes, for help with photographing of MSS. in Addis Ababa.

The staff of Makerere University College Library, Kampala.

Mlle. Simone Wallon, a Librarian at the Bibliothèque Nationale, Paris.

Mr. Hugh Tracey, Director of the International Library of African Music, Roodeport.

5. Mr. and Mrs. D. Belshaw, Mr. and Mrs. F. Dawson, and my parents, without whose hospitality in Kampala, Addis Ababa, and England the writing of the book could not have been achieved; and my wife, whose constant help and encouragement made the whole work possible.

The book is a revised form of a dissertation submitted to Durham University in January 1964. I should like to express my thanks to Professor Arthur Hutchings, Professor of Music, for his help, and to the University authorities for their agreeing to the publication of the work in book form. The original dissertation is lodged with the University Library.

Thanks are due to Mr. Richard Pankhurst for permission to quote from *Ethiopia: A Cultural History* by Sylvia Pankhurst; to Librairie Delagrave for permission to quote from the article 'La Musique éthiopienne' by C. Mondon-Vidailhet in Lavignac and La Laurencie: *Encyclopédie de la Musique*; and to the Oxford University Press for permission to quote from Ullendorff: *The Ethiopians* and Budge: *Legends of our Lady Mary the Perpetual Virgin and her Mother Hannah.*

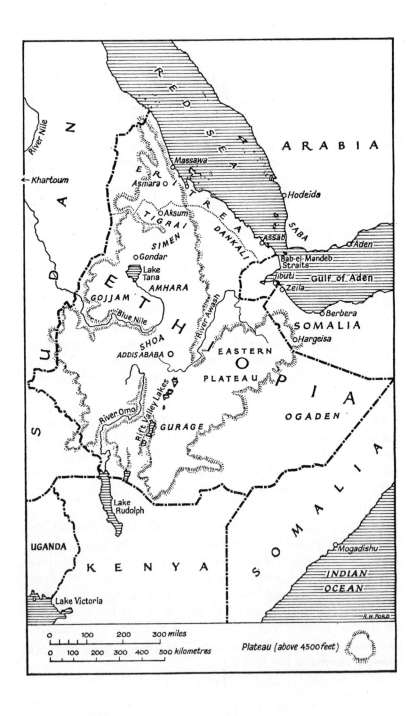

Plateau (above 4500 feet)

Introduction

Mondon-Vidailhet prefaces his article on Ethiopian music—
the only substantial account of the subject hitherto published
—with words of warning about the need to acclimatize
oneself to Ethiopian music before attempting to pass judgement on it.[1]

If it is necessary for us to judge the music of Ethiopia according to the
reputation that has been given to it by travellers, by explorers and
even by scholars, beginning with Ludolf (*Historia Aethiopiae*, 1681)
it will seem paradoxical for us to occupy ourselves with it.

The Fathers of the Company of Jesus, who were the first to speak
of it, or at any rate are the first whose opinions we have been able to
collect, treat it in the most scornful of manners. 'Although the
Abyssinians,' they say, 'play various instruments, and in singing cry
aloud as much as they can, the listener will not know how to adapt
his ears to their music.' Such is the judgement, somewhat lacking in
enthusiasm, I realize, that we find in the Bulletin of the Acts of the
Company for the year 1624–5. But, severe though we may think
this judgement is, it has not seemed too unjust to the various travellers
who have given us details about Ethiopian subjects.

His fellow-Europeans in Ethiopia were 'profoundly
astonished' when he suggested 'that Ethiopian music
deserved to excite one's interest, in particular the religious
music, which their ears seemed particularly unwilling to
accept'. But antipathy is by no means a one-sided affair:
'the Japanese and the Chinese are just as lacking in enthusiasm for our music as we are for theirs'. What he says in

---

[1] The extracts in this Introduction are from pp. 3179–80 of the article 'La
musique éthiopienne' (see Bibliography).

passing of the Far-Eastern cultures is true also of Ethiopian
culture. 'Perhaps there is fundamentally the same divergence
between their conception of musical aesthetics and ours as
the divergence that exists between their ideal in painting
and sculpture and the ideal that we conceive for ourselves.'

Thus, we must fill in the background with details of the
country's history, geography, and ethnography; for a
people's aesthetics surely grow out of their environment as
much as out of their heritage, and we must know a little
about these factors.

These remarks are reinforced by Egon Wellesz, in the
Introduction to Volume I of the *New Oxford History of
Music*.[1]

When we come to deal with non-European music we cannot apply
the same criteria as we use in studying and appreciating the music
of the West. . . . The factor of time which governs the structure of
Western music plays hardly any part in Oriental music. An Arabic
song may last more than an hour, the performance of a Chinese opera
stretch out over several days. To the Western musician conciseness of
expression, clearly shaped form, and individuality are the highest
criteria by which a work of art is judged; the attitude of the listener
is an active one: he listens to what the composer has to say. The
Eastern musician likes to improvise on given patterns, he favours
repetitions, his music doesn't develop, does not aim at producing
climaxes, but it flows; and the listener becomes entranced by the
voice of the singer, by the sound of the instruments, and by the
drumming rhythms. . . .

The main obstacle for the European listener in appreciating Far-
Eastern music comes in the beginning from the different method of
voice production. For the European, singing is a kind of elated speech;
for the Far-Eastern musician singing is opposed to speech: the voice
is used like a highly strung instrument.

Wellesz here is writing specifically of Far-Eastern music;
but his comments are entirely relevant, as later sections of
this work will help to show. Without a distinct effort of

[1] London, 1957, pp. xviii and xix.

mind to put our European concepts far away, judgement of Ethiopian music—whether of secular song and dance, folksongs with instrumental accompaniment, woodwind or string solos, or church chanting—becomes almost impossible. Mondon-Vidailhet says that the Ethiopians 'have an ancient civilization, a general culture which is connected with ours on so many sides . . . that the Abyssinians seem to us like an European island lost in a complete sea of African barbarism.' Yet their music in some respects is further removed from our musical concepts than is the music of many other parts of Africa.

This divergence between Ethiopian music and what one may call the true African music is seen particularly in the sound of the Ethiopian's singing voice. He or she speaks as pleasantly as one could wish, but the same person's voice in song strikes our ears jarringly—if we pay too much attention to the sound itself, which is of minor importance to an Ethiopian in appreciating a song. Yet the sound of most African singing is by no means displeasing. On the other hand, music from Central, South, East, and West Africa is often of extreme rhythmic complexity, contrasting with notable simplicity of rhythm in Ethiopian music. Perhaps musical developments in Europe in recent decades permit the assertion that this African rhythmic turbulence does not offend our ears: it would have done in earlier years. The Ethiopian simplicity—we might be tempted to call it sterility if we keep our European concepts—may well seem monotonous if we pay too much attention to it.

We must remember that for an Ethiopian, as for most Africans, music is something that is always encouraging him to participate. Seldom can he sit still and just listen. 'An inactive audience passively enjoying itself does not exist.'[1] In one respect this is not entirely true of Ethiopia today. A sophisticated audience in the capital might quietly and passively appreciate a love song or a lament in the

---

[1] F. Bose, *Musikalische Völkerkunde*, p. 42.

concert hall. But the same singer, the same song, in a village would invariably attract an active audience. They would join in the chorus, they would clap their hands, they would feel spontaneously every emotion of the singer. 'It is uncommon for the African to play *for* someone: he would rather play *with* someone'[1]—or sing *with* his companions, not *to* an audience.

An unfamiliar feature of Ethiopian music—but entirely acceptable, it is to be hoped—is the spontaneity, certainly of the folk music. 'The song seems to develop spontaneously and with a joyfulness which does not leave the Westerner unmoved. Where in Europe has he met this pressing desire to sing? Seldom in everyday life or in school, and not always in church.'[2]

Mondon-Vidailhet draws our attention also to the notable individuality of Ethiopian music:

One of the most important scientific missions that has been sent to Abyssinia, that of Th. Lefebvre, Petit, and Quentin-Dillon,[3] deals with Ethiopian music in a somewhat more favourable manner, in the account which accompanies the story of this interesting expedition. 'The music of the Abyssinians,' they say in it, 'is monotonous, like that of the Indians, from which it appears to come; but when one is sufficiently well instructed to be able to understand the words which this music accompanies, one cannot fail to find a certain charm in it.' . . In any case, and whatever appreciations might have been given of Abyssinian music by travellers that one has listened to, it cannot be denied that it exists with a very marked character of its own—*et c'est déjà quelque chose.*

The 'very marked character of its own' is being covered over all too quickly in the 1960s with a veneer of western musical idiom. As the country steps out of the Middle Ages

---

[1] *African Music and the Church in Africa,* by Henry Weman (Uppsala, 1960), p. 20.
[2] Ibid., p. 17.
[3] A French expedition that was in the country from 1839 to 1843, and published many volumes of findings in a wide variety of fields.

with fine enthusiasm, its music is being diversified or even lost as quickly as has European folk music been spoilt in the twentieth century. Without doubt the contacts of one sort or another that the Ethiopians have had with other peoples through more than 2,500 years of history must have had very great effects on their music. The discovery of these effects would be a fascinating, even if difficult, task, buried as they are beneath successive layers of assimilation, submission, and isolation.

The force of those last few words will be appreciated as the reader studies Chapter I of this book, where the general background of the country is sketched from various angles. After the main body of the book has dealt with the secular and church music of Ethiopia, in the last chapter the reader is again reminded of the growing danger that the true Ethiopian culture (not only the musical culture) will be submerged by the tide of twentieth-century advancement. All too soon the assimilation may be complete, the individuality lost, in secular music if not in sacred.

Research is needed at once, therefore, if the opportunity is not to be lost of discovering the relation between Ethiopian music and other eastern music, as it developed through the centuries stemming from Solomon.

1 *The Background*

(a) Geography

Ethiopia and Eritrea together form the Imperial Ethiopian Empire, a political entity that within its borders encompasses 400,000 square miles of topography noted for its contrasts.

Parts of Ethiopia, where the Danakil live, are below sea level: yet three-quarters of the population live on a vast plateau averaging between seven and eight thousand feet about sea level. In parts near the Red Sea no rain ever falls: in the south-west highlands the annual rainfall is four times London's figure. The Blue Nile flows out of the highlands and helps to water Sudan and Egypt before completing its two thousand miles to the Mediterranean: but the country's second major river, the Awash, floods down from the plateau for only a few hundred miles before it soaks away into the desert of the Red Sea littoral, never to reach the coast. Ethiopia's sea ports are among the hottest places in the world: but it also has many mountain ranges rising to fourteen and fifteen thousand feet, where dense hail may lie for days on end.

Ethiopia may be placed exactly with its neighbours by recording that it lies between 4° and 18° north of the Equator; Kenya is its southern border; Somalia is to the east and south-east; Sudan is on the west and north-west borders; and five hundred miles of the Red Sea are its north-east shores. Arabia is only twenty miles away across the Straits of Bab-el-Mandeb. At its widest, the country is about nine hundred miles across, and from north to south it is perhaps a thousand miles long.

[1]

Two-thirds of the country are occupied by a huge mountain massif. This is sharply split by the Great Rift Valley which, with the Awash River and a chain of lakes, sweeps from the Red Sea down into Central Africa. The eastern plateau is inhabited mainly by Somali and Galla people. It is on the central and northern plateau that we find the people usually thought of as the true Abyssinians or Ethiopians—the people with whose music this book is primarily concerned.

The traveller who attempts to cut from east to west across central Ethiopia faces formidable barriers. Crossing the coastal deserts and then the steamy lowlands of the Rift Valley, he is confronted by a tremendous escarpment, jumping almost sheer up six thousand feet or more and running for hundreds of miles north and south. At the top he is in a temperate climate, crossing a fertile plateau that undulates pleasantly—except that every few miles it is jagged by river chasms fifteen hundred feet deep or more. To the north he can see the Simen peaks, rising to fifteen thousand feet and occasionally snow-clad. His path is blocked by the Blue Nile gorge, ten miles wide and over three thousand feet deep. Nearing the western edge of the plateau the land falls gradually, finally reaching a lesser escarpment dropping to the torrid lowlands of the White Nile.

All these geographical features have played their part in the history of the country and its peoples. They have hindered the would-be invader and been a bulwark to the settled people. They have directly affected the music to be found there, preventing its constant dilution with the cultures of the Arabic-speaking peoples and the true African races that entirely surround Ethiopia.

Mondon-Vidailhet is not to be judged too fanciful when he sees these violent contrasts reflected in the music of the plateau people.[1]

---

[1] Mondon-Vidailhet, p. 3179.

I believe there is in a people's music something that is fitted to their particular genius, I would say almost fitted to the physical circumstances of their country; and, to confine myself to the Abyssinians, I find it in the violent side-steps (*'écarts'*) which break the ordinary monotony of their chants. Therein I find their character, made in the image of their immense plateaux which, seen from some summit, resemble infinite plains and which, when you try to cross them, surprise you at every moment with giddy descents and breath-taxing climbs. The moral reflection of this is seen in the character of the people, created with the most disconcerting contrasts, and even in the habits of the wild animals of this region.

(b) Definitions

Before details are filled in of the racial and historical background against which Ethiopian music has to be studied, some definitions must be established. ' "Ethiopia" was a name very loosely employed by the Greeks, and applied to anywhere south and east of Egypt, even as far as India.'[1] A more exact geographical use of the name 'Ethiopia' has been possible ever since the first European contacts with the country in the sixteenth century,[2] although the country's boundaries as they are now to be found on the map of Africa have altered considerably through the centuries. The people have constantly been known either as Abyssinians or as Ethiopians. In 1684 Job Ludolphus wrote: 'They are now generally called the Habessines, by others Abessines or Abessenes, the name being given to them by the Arabians. . . . They rather choose to call themselves . . . Itjopiawjan, Ethiopians, assuming the name from the Greeks. . . . The name is applied to all the swarthy-complexioned people in Asia as well as to the Blacks of Ethiopia.'[3]

Likewise, their country has had two names—or three, if the biblical 'Cush' is included.

---

[1] Pankhurst, p. 31.
[2] See section (c) of this chapter.
[3] *A New History of Ethiopia*, quoted by Pankhurst, p. 28.

The derivation of these names has been a source of much confusion, helping to obscure the origins of the people and their culture. For instance, some suggest that 'Abyssinia' is a corruption of 'Habeshat', the name of a Semitic tribe from South Arabia, while others say it derives from an Arabic word meaning 'of mixed origins'. Perhaps that is why today's Ethiopian hates being called an Abyssinian. One authority[1] denies that 'Ethiopia', as commonly supposed, comes from a Greek word meaning 'burnt faces'; he maintains its roots are in a word meaning 'incense', Ethiopia being a traditional source of this wood. Further, he supposes the derivation of 'Abyssinia' to be from a Mahri (South Semitic) word meaning 'gatherers'.

An 'Ethiop' even in Shakespeare's day was equated with a person from the Nile Valley, or Nubia, of very dark complexion. Hence we have

Away, you Ethiop!

in *Twelfth Night*, used as a term of scorn for the blackest of men, and

As black as an Ethiop

in *A Merchant of Venice*. Shakespeare was using the name as he found it in the Old Testament, although by his day the Ethiopians had been established as a plateau people, of light complexion and Semitic features, for more than fifteen hundred years, and not a lowlands negroid people.

Most authorities are now agreed that 'Ethiopia' may reasonably be used to name the whole political unit described in the preceding section; and that the true Ethiopians, culturally and ethnologically, are the majority of the inhabitants of the central and northern plateau. Of course, millions more people may call themselves Ethiopians on their passports, but they are not the real carriers of the age-old Ethiopian culture. This book does not make use

---

[1] Dr. Eduard Glaser, cited by Pankhurst, p. 40.

of 'Abyssinia' or 'Abyssinian' except in quoting from other authorities. Generally in such quotations 'Abyssinian' may be taken as synonymous with 'Ethiopian' as just defined.

The music of the land of Ethiopia today that has the most striking individuality is the music of the true Ethiopian. As already quoted from Mondon-Vidailhet, 'it exists with a very marked character of its own'. The music of other regions of the country is, in general, outside the scope of this book. A full survey of all the musical cultures, of great diversity, to be found within the Islamic, Christian, pagan, Hamitic, Semitic, or negroid confines of contemporary Ethiopia would take on encyclopedic proportions.

To prevent confusion, a clear name-system of the Christian Churches must be established. Regardless of variations of nomenclature to be found in works dealing with the Eastern Churches, here the term 'Ethiopian Church' is used for what is often loosely called the 'Coptic Church', the name 'Coptic' being properly reserved for the original Coptic Church, that of Egypt based on Alexandria. Other divisions are referred to as the Armenian Church, the Syrian Church, and so on, ignoring the additional use of 'Orthodox' or 'Coptic' in their titles. But we must not forget the essential spiritual relationship of the Eastern Churches.

The national language of the country is called Amharic. The Church language, variously known as Ge'ez or Ethiopic, in this book is referred to by the latter name, the former having a musical connotation as well.

(c) History

Political developments within Ethiopia itself have had little effect on Ethiopian culture compared with the part played by Ethiopia's relations with the outside world. Although much of interest can be found in the country's domestic history, this brief survey lays more stress on external contacts.

For an Ethiopian, history begins with Solomon and the
Queen of Sheba, or Saba, one of the four main South
Arabian states of Old Testament times.[1] The Ethiopians
hold as a cardinal element of patriotic historical faith the
belief that the Queen bore Solomon a son after she had gone
to pay homage to him, and named the son Menelik. From
Menelik, they say, the Solomonic dynasty that still holds
the throne today is directly descended. The story is en-
shrined in the *Kebra Negast*, 'The Glory of the Kings', an
early fifteenth-century manuscript supposedly translated
from a Coptic original found before A.D. 325 among the
treasures of St. Sophia of Constantinople.[2] It has been
suggested[3] that there is evidence that the Queen of Sheba
lived only after Solomon's death, but this is anathema to
the Ethiopians. 'Even if The Book makes no reference (to
her son Menelik) it is none the less probable that Solomon
had relations with Sheba, since everyone knows his inclina-
tions were such'.[4] As Ullendorff says, 'the historical fiction
of an uninterrupted line of kings descended from . . . King
Solomon and the Queen of Sheba . . . must be one of the
most powerful and influential national sagas anywhere in
the world'.[5] Be this as it may, there is no doubt of the
strength of contacts between South Arabia and Ethiopia
over a period of at least a thousand years.

In earliest times, the inhabitants of the plateau were
probably negroid aboriginals. These had been gradually
dispossessed by Cushitic peoples (that is, the basic Hamitic
Ethiopian stock) by the time that ancient Egypt made
trading contacts, taking out slaves, incense, and so on. But
the chief contact was with South Arabia, whence groups of

---

[1] See 1 Kings x. 1–13; also 2 Chronicles ix. 1–12 and Matthew xii. 42.
[2] *Ethiopia* by Jean Doresse, trans. Coult (London, 1959).
[3] In *A History of Ethiopia*, by A. H. M. Jones and E. Munroe (London,
1955).
[4] Attributed by Doresse to a nineteenth-century Tigré historian.
[5] Ullendorff, p. 64.

settlers came during a period stretching at least from the seventh century B.C. to the fourth century A.D. The fact that Ethiopia, alone among all the African states (except the Arab countries), has its own system of writing, reaching back through at least two thousand years, stems directly from the arrival of these immigrants. They brought with them a vastly superior civilization, both materially and culturally. The implications of the existence, for such a span of time, of an Ethiopian written culture are immense.

The settlers based on Aksum, in the northern plateau, gained pre-eminence over all other groups, and Aksum's power increased so greatly that in the sixth century A.D. the Aksumites invaded and subjugated South Arabia, the land whence they had originated.

The Ethiopians in the historical sense then represent the amalgam of a relatively thin layer of Semitic settlers from south-west Arabia with the great mass of the existing Cushitic population. While the colonizers from Asia very largely lost their ethnic identity, their political, social and cultural institutions now became the heritage of the population as a whole. Numerically the South Arabian leaven was not significant, but its superior quality revolutionized life in the Abyssinian highlands and infused into the predominant Cushitic element that peculiarly Semitic ingredient which has throughout the ages given Ethiopian civilization its special character.[1]

Groups of Jewish settlers also came up to the plateau, people from Jewish colonies in South Arabia with 'a peculiarly Hebraic brand of Semitism'. Their descendants may still be found in one small area in northern Ethiopia, and are known as the Falashas, or Ethiopian Jews, a quasi-fossilized relic of Judaism.

Aksum maintained its Arabian contacts, and expanded trade with Egypt through the Nile valley. Egypt now being thoroughly hellenized, Ethiopia came into direct touch with Greek civilization. The contact has lasted ever since, even if tenuously at times. King Erzana, when Aksum

---

[1] Ibid., p. 51.

was at its zenith of power and achievement, was converted to Christianity in A.D. 327. Henceforth Ethiopia's association with other Christian countries was always through Alexandria, the Coptic Church, and the Greek Orthodox Church.

A.D. 570 saw the birth of the prophet Mohammed, and the rapid growth of Muslim power followed. Nascent Islam quickly occupied the whole of Arabia, and then of North Africa. Ethiopia was thus cut off from Alexandria and lost its supply of fresh settlers from Arabia. 'The isolation of Abyssinia, which was to last for many centuries, had now begun. Trade and conquest were a thing of the past, and in the face of the great Islamic expansion there was nothing left to the people but to retire within their impregnable mountain fastness'.[1] In *Decline and Fall of the Roman Empire* (Chap. 47) Gibbon has a taut phrase to sum up the situation:

Encompassed on all sides by the enemies of their religion, the Aethiopians slept near a thousand years, forgetful of the world by whom they were forgotten.

In succeeding centuries, as Islam spread along the coasts of the Red Sea and the horn of Africa, the Ethiopians began to expand southwards over the plateau. In the tenth, eleventh, and twelfth centuries the Muslims began to encroach on the lowest parts of the plateau in the east and south, where they halted for several centuries. As Emperor Menelik II himself said in 1891, his country was 'for more than fourteen centuries an island of Christians in the midst of a sea of pagans'.[2] In the mid-thirteenth century a new king came to the Ethiopian throne, named Lalibala, from whose reign can be dated first the restoration of the Solomonic dynasty after a period of internecine strife, second a notable literary and general cultural renaissance, and third the almost complete fusion of church and state. As Ethiopian

---

[1] Ullendorff, p. 57.
[2] *The Real Abyssinia*, by C. F. Rey (London, 1935).

fortunes improved in later centuries, Lebna Dengel (1508–40) came to the throne. His reign was marked by 'two events of transcendent importance to the history of Ethiopia: the climax of the Muslim struggle with the Christian Empire culminating in the virtual occupation of the Abyssinian highlands, and Ethiopia's entry into relations with Europe in general and Portugal in particular.'[1] The King had asked for Portuguese aid against the Muslim threat, but before he could take advantage of it the terrible Imam, Ahmad ibn Ibrahim, nicknamed Gragne (the Left-handed), invaded the plateau in 1529, and by 1533 had subdued all Ethiopia.

The holocaust enveloped most parts of Ethiopia and brought in its train misery and murder, ruin and devastation. Much of the literary and intellectual heritage of Abyssinia was irretrievably lost, and the barbarism and brutality had an effect far transcending that age. To Ethiopians a good deal of their hard-won civilization was destroyed, while to the historian and *éthiopisant* precious documentation and irreplaceable evidence perished for ever.[2]

When at last Lebna Dengel received a contingent of Portuguese soldiers, Gragne was slain in 1541, the Muslims were defeated, the danger was removed—but not the damage. 'Salvation had come at a very late hour: Ethiopia lay prostrate and exhausted; many of its churches and monasteries existed no longer; its clergy was weakened, and its people were either Islamized—however superficially —or terrorized and in urgent need of moral and material succour.'[3]

By the middle of the sixteenth century a new danger had arisen. The Galla tribes were being pushed out of their lands in the horn of Africa by Somali and Danakil pressure, and inexorably they forged up on to the Ethiopian highlands. They came in huge numbers, and settled over the entire plateau except for the northern area, the region of the

---

[1] Ullendorff, p. 71.   [2] Ibid., p. 73.   [3] Ibid., p. 75.

old Aksumite kingdom.[1] 'The Gallas had nothing to contribute to the civilization of Ethiopia; they possessed no material or intellectual culture, and their social organization was at a far lower stage of development than that of the population among whom they settled.'[2]

Some Portuguese had stayed in Ethiopia after the defeat of the Muslims, maintaining a link with Roman Catholicism. As a result, a later King, Susenyos, was early in the seventeenth century received into the Roman Catholic faith, by a Spanish father of the Society of Jesus. Such a public outcry resulted that he had to recant. All foreigners were expelled from Ethiopia as a potential bad influence; suspicion of Europeans in general soon followed; and the xenophobia which lasted until only a few decades ago was well established. Once again, Ethiopia was isolated, except for its contacts with the Coptic Church, and it was not until the great era of colonial expansion in the nineteenth century that any exchange of value took place between Europe and Ethiopia.

Britain clashed with Ethiopia in the 1860s, and a British army brought back to England large numbers of manuscripts and valuable cultural materials, now mostly housed in the British Museum. Much recent study of Ethiopian culture has been based upon these items. Italy and Ethiopia also clashed, Ethiopia heavily defeating the Italians in the 1890s and the Italians occupying Ethiopia from 1935 to 1941. We thus arrive at the situation twenty years ago, when, isolationism and suspicion forgotten, Ethiopia stood 'with one leg in the United Nations, the other in the Middle Ages', to adapt C. F. Rey's phrase.[3]

---

[1] They even spread far southwards into what are now the sovereign states of Uganda, Burundi, and Ruanda. Because of this, and of Aksum conquests a thousand years before, some Ethiopians claim that in bygone days their Empire covered Arabia and much of East Africa; but this is, to say the least, a distortion both of geography and of time.

[2] Ullendorff, p. 76.

[3] *The Real Abyssinia*, p. 9.

(d) Ethnography

'L'Abissinia è un museo di popoli'[1]—there are at least seventy languages and two hundred dialects in the country, according to Rey,[2] representing as many different tribes with widely divergent cultural heritages. But we could not rightly call the country a museum of cultures as well, most of the peoples having nothing that compares with the proper Ethiopian culture. The provision of a few ethnic details, in addition to those already outlined in the preceding section, will complete this background sketching of the Ethiopian cultural scene in the twentieth century.

About one-third of the probable twelve million inhabitants of Ethiopia today are properly called Ethiopians, the peoples of Tigre, Amhara, and Gojjam in the north highlands and of Shoa in the central highlands. The major part of the remaining plateau dwellers are branches of the Gallas, whose tribes number over two hundred. The western borders of the country are occupied by negro and negroid peoples, usually known as Shankallas. The east is dominated by Muslim peoples, the Danakil, Issa, and other Somali races. To the south-east there are the Ogaden Somalis, in southern Ethiopia the Gurages (a semi-Semitic people), and near the Simen Mountains in the north there are the Falashas, or Ethiopian Jews.[3]

In brief, we find that the true Ethiopians are the Ethiopians of the main highlands. They are still perhaps 80 per cent. Hamitic, from the Hamitic peoples that arrived between 3,000 and 1,000 B.C. They have a strong leavening, especially culturally, from successive Semitic immigrations from 700 B.C. to A.D. 400. There are Hamitic Galla additions from the fifteenth and sixteenth centuries. Culturally they

---

[1] *L'Abissinia,* by C. Conti Rossini (Rome, 1929), p. 20.
[2] *The Real Abyssinia,* p. 35.
[3] See *Races of Africa,* by Seligman (London, 1939), pp. 114ff.

owe most to their Semitic Sabaean ancestors, but other lesser influences have been at work through the centuries. The living Amharic language of the plateaux, and the dead Ethiopic language of the Christian Church throughout the country, are both of the same Semitic origin.

2 *Musical Instruments*

In this chapter details are given of the musical instrument to be found in use in Ethiopia today. I have also added note of instruments (quoted by earlier authorities) which seem no longer to be in general use. The information is in most cases gathered in the following order for each instrument:

1. Description, typical size, method of construction, materials.
2. Manner of playing.
3. Use.
4. Pitch, tuning.
5. Comparison with other instruments.

Only one of the instruments (the sistrum) has a purely sacred use. Some of the others are used in church but also have their place in secular music.

Most of the instruments that I studied were either in the Museum of the Institute of Ethiopian Studies, Haile Selassie I University, Addis Ababa, or in the folklore orchestra of the Haile Selassie I Theatre, Addis Ababa. These two sources are referred to as 'the Museum' and 'the Orchestra' respectively. Some of the Museum instruments originated in the provinces, but where the origin is not given they were manufactured in Addis Ababa, where, the Curator of the Museum said, 'we know some wandering musicians, who themselves make the instruments'.

(a) Percussion Instruments

The *Negarit* is a type of kettledrum. It is normally hemispherical in section, sometimes with the base of the

hemisphere sliced off to give a small flat bottom. The body is made of wood, silver, or gold. The skin is some sort of animal hide, usually of ox, and in many cases the skin covers the whole instrument, being sewn together and tensioned latitudinally round the middle of the body.

There are three examples of negarit in the Museum. Two of them (the left-hand and middle ones) may be seen in Plate 2. Their measurements are given below, beginning with the left-hand one.

Catalogue No.	Diameter of top	Overall depth
80	47 cm.	18 cm.
—	46 cm.	15 cm.
1753	34 cm.	7 cm.

Each of the three has a wooden body, hollowed out of a single section of tree-trunk. The first two both have an integral wooden handle projecting about an inch on one side, through which a carrying strap may be passed.

The measurements indicate that the negarit is surprisingly large in diameter for its depth. Examples of greater diameter exist, perhaps up to 70 cm., but they are not more than 45 cm. or 50 cm. in depth.

The negarit is always played with a wooden stick or mallet, never with the hands. It is sometimes beaten with two sticks, sometimes with one, depending on whether the player has one or two drums in use. It is impressively sonorous, and, of course, of varying pitch according to size. Once made, the negarit is not tuned: the pitch appears remain sufficiently constant to satisfy the player.

The instrument is entirely a ceremonial one, 'one of distinctive emblems of authority'.[1] The Emperor's ne would be made of gold; senior officials would have ones; the wooden ones would be for lesser but still in

---

[1] The quotations about this instrument are from Mondon-Vidail

government officials. During the Emperor's progress on some ceremony of state, the negarits would be borne on mules before him. Each rider, seated almost on the animal's haunches, would have a pair of drums slung from the saddle. The fact that they are often mule-borne probably accounts for their shallow draught: they would be too unwieldy, and too heavy if deeper.[1]

The name derives from the root 'nagara', which means 'he spoke', and in effect every proclamation, every public order is preceded by one or more drum-beats. For royal proclamations, which are read outside the palace gates, the negarit is beaten forty times. . . . In other circumstances the drum-beating takes place on the rug-strewn terrace where the sovereign is installed to dispense justice, one of his special attributes. . . . The rank of an official can be recognized by the form of the negarit, but above all by the number of drummers who precede him. When the Emperor comes to the army he is preceded by 88 drums, carried by 44 mules. . . A Ras, who has the highest rank in the kingdom after the sovereign, has 44 drums as the sign of his authority: the Dedjazmatch, who comes after the Ras, has 22, or a number equal to the number of districts he governs. The negarit is also beaten at the funerals of members of the imperial family, and in great ceremonies.

Ceremonial uses of the negarit such as Mondon-Vidailhet describes, writing some sixty years ago, are declining in number today. However, in the Silver Jubilee celebrations of the present Emperor, Haile Selassie I, held in 1955, a large contingent of negarits preceded the Emperor in the state procession through the streets of the capital. They did not seem to beat in consort according to any fixed pattern, but rather to make an impressive volume of sound, alternating with the playing of the imperial trumpets, or *malakats*.[2]

---

[1] In medieval Europe there were similar shallow drums called knackers. These were either slung in pairs from the player's waist, resting against his thighs, or were hung from the shoulders of a man who walked in front of the player.

[2] See section (b) (iii) of this chapter.

The third instrument in the Museum, the one which has no handle, and which is of notably smaller size, probably would be for an official of low rank, and would be played while it stood on the ground or rested on the striker's hip or lap.

It is interesting to find that what Mondon-Vidailhet describes for the use of the negarit only six decades ago is, by and large, just what was the case four centuries ago. In 1520 Alvares wrote that the negarit drums were a symbol of authority, the importance of the officer being indicated by the number of drums. 'The drum is carried on the back of a mule. . . . By beating it people's attention is called in the market place to announce a punishment or to issue an order of the governor.'[1]

We see here only one of many examples of the permanence of tradition in Ethiopia through century after century as the nation remained cut off in its mountain inaccessibility.

(ii) The *Kabaro* is another type of kettledrum. It is fairly tall, and often slender. The body is made of a hollowed-out section of tree-trunk, and has a roughly cylindrical shape, truncated at both ends. Mondon-Vidailhet says that the body may be in 'silver or even gold, according to the riches of the churches or the generosity of the donors'.[2] The exact shape of the body seems to be determined by the shape of the chosen trunk, rather than by any established norm. In general, the body tapers towards the bottom. Some kabaros have circular heads, some are almost oval. Ox-hide is stretched over each end, the skins being laced together and tautened by a pattern of thongs that is more or less decorative (at the will of the maker, usually a debtera or church musician) as well as functional.

Three examples are kept in the Museum, of varying shapes and sizes, and their dimensions are given below.

---

[1] *The Prester John of the Indies* by Fr. Francisco Alvares, trans. Lord Stanley of Adderley (Cambridge, 1961).
[2] The extracts in this description come from pp. 3183–4.

The fourth instrument detailed here is one actually in use in Holy Trinity Cathedral, Addis Ababa.

Catalogue No.	Origin	Height	Cylin-drical or tapering	Oval or round head	Size of top head	Size of bottom head
831	Addis Ababa	38 cm.	cylindrical	round	26 cm. diam.	26 cm. diam.
1884	—	32 cm.	cylindrical	oval	24 × 22 cm.	24 × 22 cm.
1455	—	48 cm.	tapering	oval	36 × 30 cm.	24 × 22 cm.
	Holy Trinity	75 cm.	tapering	round	46 cm. diam.	25 cm. diam.

The kabaro player in the Orchestra makes use of a number of different-sized instruments, ranging from perhaps 38 cm. to 60 cm. in height. In some churches kabaros may be found that stand as high as 90 cm.

The kabaro is played with the hands, and only seldom with a stick. If the player is striking both ends, the drum is slung round his neck and hangs diagonally in front of him, slightly on his left side (see Plate 1). The larger end is uppermost, and is struck with the right hand, while the left hand plays on the smaller lower end. Mondon-Vidailhet says that 'in church, when it is desired to increase the sonorousness, the kabaro is suspended in some sort of framework'. At times, the instrument is stood on the floor on its narrower end, and only the deeper-sounding top head is played.

In general, the kabaro is 'the kettledrum reserved for religious ceremonies'; but as already mentioned it is used in the folklore orchestra at the Haile Selassie Theatre. It may be found in use in some villages for popular folk music, although the drum more generally used for traditional music

[17]

is the *atamo*.[1] It appears that the Orchestra uses the kabaro because of its resonance, and its greater suitability for supporting an ensemble of ten or a dozen instruments, rather than because of its popularity as a secular instrument.

The name comes from the root 'he was honourable', and the kabaro is an instrument that is particularly honoured. . . . In the processions, the kabaro accompanies the tabernacle, wherein is placed, under rich cloths, the portable altar, or *tabot*, which takes the place in Ethiopia of the monstrance, or ostensory, of our priests.

The kabaro serves as the accompaniment for Abyssinian plainchant. Struck with the hands, with a particular skill, producing sounds that are sometimes sharp and abrupt, sometimes muffled or restrained, it punctuates the long plainchants of the liturgy or marks the rhythm of the religious dances.

As is the case with the negarit, the tuning of the drum-heads of the kabaro is not altered, once the instrument has been made. Even when the two heads are the same size, the skin of the lower one is stretched more tightly than the upper skin, so that the instrument produces the same alternating tenor and bass sounds as does a tapering kabaro. The tenor skin (the lower one) on a tapering instrument may be stretched more tightly, proportionately, than the upper or bass skin. This has the effect of increasing the distance between the pitch of the two notes rather more than would be achieved merely by having one head smaller than the other.

Drums in one shape or another are common to nearly every culture in the world, but the double-ended type like the kabaro is not at all common. Early in the nineteenth century Villoteau compared it with the Turkish drum, the 'tabit tourki'.[2] This might lead to the establishing of a definite cultural influence stretching through Islamic lands, but it would be a laborious task to trace it. Moreover, since the simple drum is a frequently found instrument, there is

---

[1] See section (a) (iii) of this chapter.
[2] *Description de l'Egypte* (Paris, 1808).

[18]

no reason why two widely separated peoples should not independently develop the two-headed drum.

When used in church services, to accompany the chanting or dancing, the kabaro is played in one of three distinct rhythmic patterns, with or without the sistrum chinking and the prayer sticks thumping on the floor.[1] Examples of each of these rhythms taken from performances at Holy Trinity Cathedral, Addis Ababa, are given overleaf (Exx. 1–3).

(iii) The *Atamo* is a drum small enough to be held in the hand or under the arm. The body usually is made of baked earthenware pottery, although Mondon-Vidailhet says it is made of wood.[2] Usually the atamo has inside it some small stones, pieces of broken pot, or seeds. As with the kabaro and negarit, there is no fixed size. An idea of the divergent measurements is given by the following details of the instruments in the Museum.

Catalogue No.	Pot or Wood	Depth	Diameter of head	No. of stones/seeds
824	pot	20 cm.	20 cm.	1
1150	pot	15 cm.	19 cm.	many
948	pot	11·5 cm.	18 cm.	many
1132	wood	25 cm.	oval, 32 × 25 cm.	none
1687/1705	pot	30 cm.	oval, 42 × 33 cm.	none

824 is from the Borana, a tribe in south-east Ethiopia. 1150 is from Wollega province, in the western highlands. 948 is a Gurage instrument, and may have come from any of the many parts of the plateau where these people have settled. It is shown in Plate 8. 1687/1705 may be seen in Plate 6 —it is the middle instrument in the bottom row. It is of excessive size, both in weight and overall measurements,

---

[1] See section (a) (vii) of this chapter; also Chap. 4 (f).
[2] His references to the instrument may be found on p. 3184.

Ex. 1

Ex. 2

Ex. 3

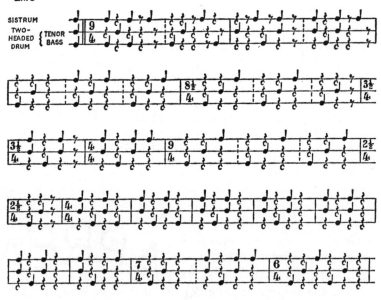

Ex. 3 has been barred quite arbitrarily. The sequence of beats seems to be dictated by the rhythm of the words of the text, and there is no obvious recurrent pattern.

for an atamo, but its method of construction is the same as the smaller instruments. It comes from the Kambatta, a mostly pagan tribe amongst the southern lakes of the Rift Valley. It is a funeral drum. All these instruments (except 1132) have a skin stretched over the hollow of the pot, held taut by thongs or strings criss-crossing the underside of the pot.

1132, which is to be seen in the bottom right corner of Plate 6, seems to be a hybrid. Not only is it made of wood, but it also has an oval head at both top and bottom. In this respect it is like a kabaro; but its shallow draught of 25 cm., especially in relation to the large size of the drum head, makes it more like an atamo, which is what a museum guide named it to me. A kabaro with a head this size would stand between 45 cm. and 50 cm. high. This instrument came from Sidamo, a south-west plateau province.

The atamo is held under the arm or between the knees of the player. It is struck with the fingers or palm of one or both hands, in *ad libitum* rhythmic patterns the decoration of which depends entirely upon the dexterity of the exponent. However complex the embellishment, the basic rhythmic pattern is always a simple four or three beats. It is used entirely as a secular instrument, accentuating the beat of folk-song or dance, notably at weddings and family celebrations, or at big festivals. According to Mondon-Vidailhet, 'it did not seem to be in much use in Shoa, where its place has been taken by some other sonorous instrument. Moreover, a certain sentimental superstition goes with the use of the atamo, which the sorcerers use for the cure of people who have received poisonous bites; as they are convinced that the patient will die unless he is kept awake, they make a deafening noise in his ears with the drums.'

(iv) The *Dawal* is an ordinary European-type bell and as such merits little consideration here. A few examples of Ethiopian-made copies are to be found. R. E. Cheesman mentions finding 'a roughly cast metal bell' weighing about a hundredweight at the church on Kebran Island, in Lake

Tana.[1] 'Bells and handbells (*marawat*), of European manufacture, are sought after for the churches. Some bells are of
considerable size, but they are rare, and as bell-towers do
not exist they are installed on a wooden frame at the entry
to the church. They are never rung as a peal, but only the
clapper is set moving.'[2]

Little silver handbells are used in the Mass, especially
in the Sanctus.[3]

(v) The true Ethiopian bell, or *Dawal*, is a resonant slab
of stone, or, at times, a resonant spar of wood. Cheesman
found some at the same church as the rough-cast bell.
'There were also two stone bells made of pairs of narrow
slabs of rock, the longest 8 feet long by 1 foot wide, slung
by creeper-stems to wooden frames. A round pebble lies on
the top of the stones and is used as the striker. When
sounded the bells gives out two notes as each stone is struck
in turn.'[4]

Often the stones are suspended sufficiently close for one
to be able to make them sound by knocking one against the
other.[5] On Rima Island, also in Lake Tana, there is a peal
of three stone bells, the largest being 4·8 m. long by 30 cm.
thick. 'Their tones are loud and musical.'[6]

Cheesman made the most thorough exploration yet
attempted of the shores and islands of Lake Tana, with
their numerous monasteries and churches, many of which
had escaped mutilation at the Muslim invaders' hands
in the sixteenth century. He found some bell-peals of
wood.

A third kind of bell is composed of three wooden clappers, merely
shaped timber boards. The middle board is the largest and is tongue-
shaped and about 4 feet high by 2 feet wide. Two slightly smaller
clappers are loosely bound by ropes of creeper-stems to the front
and back of the middle board through two holes, and on each side.

---

[1] *Lake Tana and the Blue Nile* (London, 1936), p. 154.
[2] Mondon-Vidailhet, p. 3184.   [3] Ibid.   [4] Cheesman, op. cit., p. 154.
[5] Mondon-Vidailhet, p. 3184.   [6] Cheesman, op. cit., p. 169.

The middle board has a stout handle and a man can make a clapping noise by shaking the whole concern.[1]

This type of wooden or stone bell provides an important link with Byzantine and Coptic culture. 'Such bells were common in the monasteries in Egypt and Syria and Meso-potamia, and they were probably introduced into Abyssinia by the Coptic monks who went there in the thirteenth century.'[2]

Plate 3 shows a peal of four stone bells with the stone striker being used.

(vi) The *Qatchel* is a small hand-rattle. The one example in the Museum (catalogue no. 703) may be seen in Plate 9, on the extreme left, and Plate 8, top right. It is made of a thin strip of metal folded over so as to form an elongated hollow cone, 6 cm. long, with a base opening of diameter 2 cm. At the top there is a little circular handle. Inside there is a thin nail-like metal striker. When shaken, it makes a distinctly metallic rattling sound that has a slight resonant quality. It was suggested to me by Tsegaye Gabre Medhin[3] that the qatchel is a cattle-bell or camel-bell. However, the Museum possesses several large and noisy wooden examples of such bells, and the small metal qatchel could hardly make sufficient noise to be effective for tracking straying animals. It seems more likely that this is the qatchel described by Mondon-Vidailhet.

In most churches in the Orient, the moment of the consecration of the Host is wrapped in a show of mysterious solemnity, which is also found in Ethiopia but in a lesser degree. I have been present at Divine Services in Jerusalem where, during the consecration, resonant hand-rattles are swung, producing a confused noise which the Oriental Christians consider to add to the solemnity which ought to accompany the accomplishment of the eucharistic mystery. The Qatchel, the Abyssinian rattle, has the same purpose and comes from the same

---

[1] Ibid., p. 154.
[2] Sir E. A. Wallis Budge, *A History of Ethiopia* (London, 1928), p. 163.
[3] Cultural Director of the Haile Selassie Theatre.

source. However, it seems to me that it is being used less frequently nowadays, and that the silver sound of the handbell is taking the place of the somewhat uncouth sounds of the qatchel, so much so that even the name is becoming synonymous with the handbell and generally has this meaning.[1]

The Curator of the Museum told me that the qatchel is not properly an item of church paraphernalia, though it may be used in church ceremonies. The common use is as a sheep-bell.

(vii) The *Ts'anats'el* is a sistrum. It usually is some 15–18 cm. high, and consists of a handle of wood surmounted by a lyre-shaped silver frame. The sides of the lyre are pierced by two or three latitudinal wires or thin metal bars, running from one side to the other. On each of these, three little metal discs are threaded. Sometimes the whole instrument is made of solid silver or gold. Plate 4 shows a typical ts'anats'el.

The ts'anats'el is held in the left hand, with the arm bent up in front of the shoulder. It is then gently shaken back and forth away from the body, in any of the three fixed rhythmic patterns already mentioned for the kabaro.[2] These rhythms are set out in Exx. 1, 2, and 3 above.

The ts'anats'el is only used in the services of the church, and has no part to play in secular music at all.

In *Grove*, we read that the sistrum was 'an ancient Egyptian form of rattle, used more especially in the worship of Isis. It consisted of a metal frame upon a handle, and through the sides of the frames loose metal bars were fitted.'[3] The Ethiopian sistrum differs from the old Egyptian type in that the latter was rounded and closed at the top, whereas the former is open, the sides forming a 'U' shape.[4]

This instrument can be traced back to great antiquity. According to Ovid, Rome received it from Egypt; it was used at the celebrations of the mysteries of Isis, the good goddess; and it is to be found

---

[1] Mondon-Vidailhet, p. 3184.   [2] See section (a) (ii) of this chapter.
[3] Vol. VII, p. 825.   [4] See Mondon-Vidailhet, p. 3184.

among the hieroglyphics with the phonetic transcription 'sekhem'. It seems that one cannot find it today outside Ethiopia, where it remains a purely liturgical instrument.[1]

Mondon-Vidailhet quotes an Ethiopian legend that attributes the use of the ts'anats'el in the services of the Church to St. Yared, the supposed inventor of Ethiopian liturgical chant.[2]

He had the idea of creating the ts'anats'el after hearing the songs of birds, and, as religious mysticism never loses its place in Ethiopia, it was as a reminder of the mystery of the Trinity that he had the idea of putting on each of the three rods of the instrument the three metallic laminas, whose unobtrusive resonance calls attention to certain parts of the service, and contributes a certain animation to these parts, for the ts'anats'el only accompanies gay music.[3]

There is a certain resemblance between the chinking of the Ethiopian sistrum and the montonous chirping that passes for birdsong in the country; but it is too fanciful to account for the invention of the whole instrument in such a manner. The legend would appear to be a rationalization, to explain the addition in the unknown past of the metal discs by the Ethiopians to the loose metal rods of the Egyptian sistrum.

(viii) These passages are quoted from Mondon-Vidailhet[4] in order to complete the record of percussive instruments as far as possible. I was not able to find any information about them from authorities consulted in Ethiopia, and their continued existence—perhaps even their original existence —may properly be doubted.

There exists an instrument called the *qanda kabaro*, or more commonly the *karabo*, which is a drum of considerably smaller size than the *negarit* or *kabaro*. Soldiers use it in certain provinces. It is placed under the arm, and beaten with the hand. It seems formerly to have enjoyed more popularity than it does today. As for the *deb ambassa*, mentioned in some ancient chronicles, it has completely disappeared.

---

[1] Ibid.   [2] See Chap. 4 (d).
[3] Mondon-Vidailhet, pp. 3184–5.   [4] pp. 3184 and 3185.

Villoteau also speaks of the *qanda*, probably the *qanda karabo* of which I have spoken above, which resembled, he says, the royal drum of Guinea and of T'aqa, consisting of a great rod of wood, iron or copper. It was struck with a little wooden mallet, and was intended to replace the bells and the resonant stones in Christian churches situated in Muslim countries. One can easily understand that this instrument may have fallen into complete disuse, the Abyssinians being master today of all the Christian countries over which their ancestors had dominion, whilst in all these territories the Muslims have become their subjects or their vassals.

(b) Wind Instruments

(i) The *Washint* is a simple flute, with four finger-holes. It is nearly always made from a length of bamboo cane, the 'chembaqo, a sort of reed or bamboo that the experts call the *phragmites isiaeus*'.[1] The details that follow are based upon information given me by Lakew Abebe[2] and upon study of the washints to be found in the Museum.

Abebe's seven or eight different washints all vary in dimension. Detailed measurements were not taken, but they varied as much as do the four examples in the Museum. These latter may be seen in Plate 5, and are described here, listed in the order in which they appear in the picture from

Catalogue number	Overall length	Distance between mouthpiece and:				Bore
		1st hole	*2nd hole*	*3rd hole*	*4th hole*	
1324	55 cm.	41 cm.	36 cm.	29 cm.	25 cm.	2·5 cm.
1759	61 cm.	49·5 cm.	45 cm.	34 cm.	30 cm.	1·75 cm.
397	33 cm.	12 cm.	9 cm.	5·5 cm.	1·5 cm.	1 cm.
979	44·5 cm.	25 cm.	19·5 cm.	14·5 cm.	9 cm.	1·5 cm.

[1] Mondon-Vidailhet, p. 3186.
[2] Chief washint player and leader of the Orchestra.

top to bottom. (The fifth or lowest instrument is described at the end of this chapter.)

The Museum's instruments are collected from various parts of the country, and are not made especially for display. Variations in the distances between the finger-holes, and in other respects too, are to be expected in view of the rule-of-thumb method of construction explained below. It was not possible to play the Museum instruments, but the detailed measurements just set out indicate that they would produce notes roughly in the scale that Abebe's instruments play, which also is explained below.

No two of Abebe's instruments look alike, neither do any of the Museum ones, as may be seen in the picture. 1324, from the south-central province of Arussi, appears to be made of bamboo, but it consists of only one segment (whereas all Abebe's consist of a length of cane with four of the rings or notches that are typical of bamboo cane). It is covered all over with fine decorative burnt marks. 1759 is a somewhat twisted piece of bamboo, and seems thinner than its length would lead one to expect. 397, which comes from Guder, west of the capital, does not seem to be made of bamboo, and is remarkably straight. It too is unsegmented. 979, from Wollo, also in the south, is decorated at the mouthpiece with thread wound tightly round it.

Mondon-Vidailhet gives no typical size for the instrument, but says 'usually it has six holes'.[1] This is not so, if Abebe's instruments and those in the Museum are true washints; which is more likely to be the case than not. Indeed, a good deal of what Mondon-Vidailhet states about the washint and also about the *embilta*, another flute,[2] in no way corresponds with the result of my researches. All the washints that I have seen have four finger-holes. None has any wind-hole such as is to be found just below the mouthpiece in a recorder. The top of the instrument is 'cut open

---

[1] p. 3186.
[2] See section (c) (ii) of this chapter; also Mondon-Vidailhet, pp. 3185–6.

as a mouthpiece, forming a right-angle, and with a thin lower edge'[1] which serves to set the air column in the instrument vibrating.

The washint is not held transversely to the mouth, as is the European flute, nor is it held as is the recorder. Its playing stance is halfway between these two, diagonally towards the player's right. 'The breath is blown into it in some sideways fashion.'[2] The sound is very like that of a recorder, but with a little more edge to it. It is quite penetrating, but pleasing.

The washint is entirely secular in use. It may be used to accompany solo or chorus songs, which may or may not be interspersed with dances, or to play solos. It is the most popular wind instrument today; it is also the most important, as the stringed instruments are tuned to it.[3] It has the greatest potentialities of the wind instruments; and to achieve a competent executant's standard is not remarkably difficult.

Naturally the pitch of each washint varies according to the overall length of the instrument, its bore, and the distance between the finger-holes and the mouthpiece. The player selects a washint that in pitch suits the tessitura of the singer he is to accompany. In explaining the scale played by the instrument, it would be misleading to speak of any particular note as being doh, as four of the five notes can each be considered the key-centre at different times. It is safer to record that, if the note produced by the full pipe (that is, with all four finger-holes closed) is arbitrarily named A, then opening the holes successively from the bottom of the instrument produces the rising note-succession A–C–D–E–G, the D being a little sharp. This sequence was the same on all Abebe's instruments. Putting it differently, the washints examined all produced a scale of notes roughly equivalent to the pentatonic or black-notes scale of the piano.

---

[1] Mondon-Vidailhet, pp. 3185–6.   [2] Ibid.
[3] See section (c) (ii) and (vi) of this chapter.

Over-blowing produced the same notes an octave higher, giving a range of ten notes available to the player.

Establishing the fact that every washint plays the same scale of notes, or should do so, led to inquiry into how the finger-holes are bored in the correct place relative to the mouthpiece and to each other. Abebe told me that he makes all his own instruments, and that his method is the one generally used. The rings or notches determine the position of the holes, the bamboo usually having segments of roughly equal length. The mouthpiece end is a half-segment.[1] Using the notches as a guide, the flute-maker cuts the first, or highest-sounding, finger-hole in the second whole segment, just below the second notch. The second hole is cut in the second whole segment, just above the third notch. In placing these two holes, care is taken that they are not evenly spaced so as to divide the second segment into three equal parts: being placed close to the notches they leave a larger gap between themselves than between the holes and the notches. The third hole comes just below the third notch, in the third whole segment, and the fourth or lowest hole just above the lowest notch, also in the third whole segment. The bottom end of the instrument is another half-segment.

If the finger-holes are named in the same arbitrary fashion as above (from the lowest, C–D–E–G) it may be seen that the spacing between C and D is a little greater than that between D and E, although C–D–E is a succession of whole tones in European scales. But as already stated the D sounds a little sharp on the washint, which means the two spacings cannot be the same. The E–G spacing may look small, but it is only three semitones and not a major third, and therefore only one and a half times greater than the space between notes a tone apart.

It was a source of surprise to Abebe that, if he were to bore another hole just below the lowest notch, and one

---

[1] This description may be more easily followed if reference is made to Plate 5, the third instrument from the top, which has its mouthpiece towards the left.

ETHIOPIAN MUSIC

between the top and second holes, he would then fill in the
gaps and be able to play something approximating to the
European minor scale. He was familiar with the sound of
such a scale, but the possible modification of his washint
had not occurred to him.

Abebe's description of his method of positioning the
finger-holes seems plausible. Yet instruments 1324 and 397
in the Museum consist of only one segment of cane, with
no rings, and the unknown makers could not have used any
method such as Abebe's. In such a blank piece of stick, the
holes could be positioned by measuring them against a
washint already made by the notch method. A player who
had made a number of his own instruments previously from
segmented cane should readily be able to position the
holes by eye, without the guiding rings. Slight variation or
inaccuracy would not matter, as it is very infrequently that
washints are played in consort. It is reasonable to suppose
that the length of segment on a piece of bamboo is generally
in a constant ratio to the thickness or bore of the pipe.
Such being the case, the washint maker is safe in relying on
the notches to guide him, not needing to consider the size
of the cane he uses.

The washint may be compared to the European flageolet,[1]
which had four finger-holes on the front or upper side and
two thumb-holes on the under side of the instrument. The
washint does not have a thumb-hole. Mondon-Vidailhet's
illustration of a washint[2] appears to be in fact a malakat,
and his description of this latter instrument corresponds
with his washint picture.[3]

The fifth or lowest Museum instrument, catalogue no.
494, (see Plate 5), comes from E. Gurage, and differs
markedly from the true washint. It has only two sections of
bamboo, is 46 cm. long and of bore 1·5 cm. The mouth-

---

[1] For a full description of this instrument, see *Grove* under 'fipple flutes'.
[2] p. 3186, fig. 737.
[3] The malakat is described at section (b) (iii) of this chapter.

[30]

piece (on the right) does not have the thin lower edge described above, but there is a vibrating-hole similar to a recorder's just below the mouthpiece. There is only one cavernous finger-hole, 4 cm. wide, at a distance of 34 cm. from the mouthpiece. The purpose of such a large opening is not plain, and it is hard to credit the information given by a museum guide that all four fingers would be used to close it. Possibly it is a shepherd-boy's rudimentary pipe on which he would play a monotonous two-note tune. Theoretically it would be possible to raise first one finger and then another, or two together, etc., of the several fingers needed to close the hole; but with the fingers very close together this would produce a succession of quarter-tones, or even smaller intervals, quite foreign to Ethiopian music. It is interesting to note that many Gurage people are either pagan or Muslim. If this instrument is played in the manner suggested, its music would have a very strong Arab flavour. On balance, this does not seem likely, as a flute-type instrument for Arabian music would not be so primitive. The shepherd-boy explanation seems the more likely one.

In a lengthy chapter on secular music, Sylvia Pankhurst dismisses the washint, along with the other flute, the embilta, in a cryptic phrase: 'the embilta is a flute, the washint, pipes'. This would appear to mean that the washint is a number of pipes fastened together, like pan-pipes. As she adds nothing to this remark, it is hard to justify it. However, in this connection Figure 1 (see next page) is of interest, as it shows a set of pan-pipes from a distant corner of Ethiopia. The instrument comes from the Male tribe, in the extreme south-west, near Lake Rudolph—an area inhabited by Nilotic-Negroid tribes.[1] Figure 2 is a drawing of a flute of the Ubamer people in the same region. It has four finger-holes and is very like the washint of the plateau. It is approximately 40 cm. long.

---

[1] Eike Haberland *et al.*, op. cit., p. 39 of the illustrated appendix.

Fig. 1. Pan-pipes

Fig. 2. Flute

Ex. 4 shows a short extract from a typical washint extemporization.

Ex.4

(ii) The *Embilta* is a larger and more primitive type of flute than the washint. None of the three examples in the Museum has any finger-holes, and it was emphatically stated by players in the Orchestra that the embilta never does have finger-holes. This completely contradicts Mondon-Vidailhet's lengthy description, partly quoted here.[1]

The fingering charts of the Ethiopian flutes vary very greatly; although the flutes used in the retinue of the Emperor, and of great personages authorized to employ them, have only one hole, the

---

[1] p. 3185.

popular flutes have a somewhat complicated tablature, forming two series from the point of view of the spacing, thus

```
    o o o   o o
   o o o o   o o o
  o o o o o   o o o
```

Mondon-Vidailhet's drawing of an embilta[1] illustrates one of these tablatures as set out here, but this description certainly does not fit any embilta of which I was able to find details, nor does it accord with the washint, today's popular flute, as described above.

The measurements of the Museum's three examples are as given here:

Catalogue No.	Length	Bore	Origin	Length of cut-out mouthpiece
838	95 cm.	2·5 cm.	Gore	7·5 cm.
1607	75 cm.	2·25 cm.	Shoa	6·5 cm.
837	77·5 cm.	2·4 cm.	Gore	no cut-out

These are the three dark-coloured instruments in the centre of Plate 6. Gore, the source of two of them, is a province in the western highlands, and Shoa is in the central highlands. 838 is bound with strips and quite broad pieces of leather or skin for nearly its whole length. 1607 is decorated with spaced-out bands of leather.

The mouthpiece cut-out section on the first two instruments results from the removal of a slice of bamboo for about one-third the width of the bore of the pipe, for the length shown in Figure 3. This leaves a 'U'-shaped mouthpiece, with

Fig. 3

an arc-shaped edge at the lower end of the mouthpiece,

[1] Ibid., fig. 736.

instead of the flat edge that is more usual in wind instruments for the breath-column to vibrate against.

The embilta is held as is the washint, that is, at a downwards angle away from the body towards the player's right.
The sound is a rounded woolly note.

The embilta is a ceremonial instrument, being grouped
with the negarit and malakat, a drum and trumpet respectively, as 'the insignia of royalty'. Being of such rudimentary
nature, it could be of little use in folk music.

A melody is played at some ceremonies by having a consort of embiltas, each able to play a different note. Each
player sounds his note at the appropriate moment, and a
tune is thus laboriously built up. Mondon-Vidailhet quotes
one of these 'melodies of the imperial embiltas'[1] (Ex. 5),

Ex. 5

and adds that this method of playing a song 'by alternation
is as was done in old Russian military music, it is said'.

The embilta is generally considered to be a genuine part
of the cultural tradition of the plateau. James Baum visited
Ras Hailu, king of the province of Gojjam, a province in
the western plateau noted for its musicality, and found the
embiltas being played in this 'alternation' method; but he
makes a puzzling statement as to the source of the melody.

Twenty of the blackest Shankalla slaves that ever were filed to the
front and struck up a weird savage tune on bamboo-reed pipes; it was
the highland chieftain's slave band. Each hollow reed gave but a single
note, and the tune was carried on by each slave waiting until the
proper instant when his own note was needed. A strange and weird
effect they made, blowing lustily, now this pipe, now that, now several
at once, then others tuning in from their places in the line, but the
whole blending together, in a wild swinging march. It was no Abyssin-

[1] p. 3185.

ian tune, that, it must have come with the slaves from the dark forests along the Sudanese borders.[1]

The Ras's Shankalla slaves certainly would have come from the hot lowlands of the Nile valley, but it is likely that he would have his band play familiar highlands music rather than their native music. 'A strange and weird effect, a wild swinging march' could well be used as a description of Ethiopian music, as well as of Shankalla slave music, and Baum was probably mistaken.

The ceremonial embilta is also called the *mecer qanna*, apparently because in former times a consort was used in the cathedral church at Aksum, particularly for the great ceremonies at the celebration of the Wedding Feast of Cana.[2]

Mondon-Vidailhet draws an interesting historical parallel in this extract.

It is strange to record that at the zenith of the Roman empire the consuls were themselves preceded by flute players, and I am sure that the appearance of Consul Diulius' retinue did not differ greatly from that of the great noblemen of Ethiopia. . . . I would not go so far as to say that Ethiopia has borrowed her flute players from Rome. But I would add that in Abyssinia, when the Emperor wishes to honour his guests particularly, he sends them some musicians (I personally have had the honour of receiving the flute players), which of course leads to their receiving suitable payment.[3]

One cannot easily account for the discrepancy between Mondon-Vidailhet's description of the embilta and the details I have given. It is not reasonable to suppose that the 'popular flute' he mentions has never existed, as he gives so many details of it. It may well still be found in some areas, although the washint, with its four finger-holes, definitely is the popular wind instrument over much of the plateau today; the embilta today is thought of as a one-note relic of the rapidly dying great ceremonial occasions.

---

[1] *Savage Abyssinia* (London, 1928), p. 193.
[2] Mondon-Vidailhet, p. 3185.   [3] Ibid.

That there used to exist—and possibly still does exist—an instrument such as Mondon-Vidailhet describes for the embilta is confirmed by one recording I made. This was taken from a tape made by the British Council in Addis Ababa. Unfortunately, the exact origin of the tape recording was not known, though probably it was made by the orchestra of the Patriotic Association in Addis Ababa. The music is played on a deep-sounding flute, with a tone almost like that of a saxophone. It is of the same florid line as is the typical washint piece. This unidentified example is set out in Ex. 6. Obviously the instrument used for this piece must

Ex.6

a solo voice then takes up the same melody

be one with at least four finger-holes, and of considerably larger size than any washint described above, because of its pitch and tonal quality. But it cannot have been played by an embilta such as I have stated here to be the true type, that is, one without finger-holes.

(iii) The *Malakat* is a type of trumpet, usually a yard or more in length. It is made of bamboo, with a bell-shaped mouth at the bottom end. This bell-shape may be made of copper, or may be a section cut from the neck of a gourd. The whole instrument is usually decorated in one way or another. The bell-mouth may be ornamented with beads

Plate 1: Kabaro

Plate 2: Negarit

Plate 3: Bell-stones

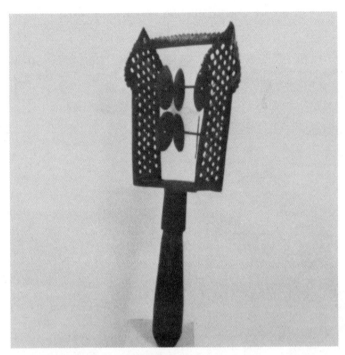

Plate 4: Sistrum

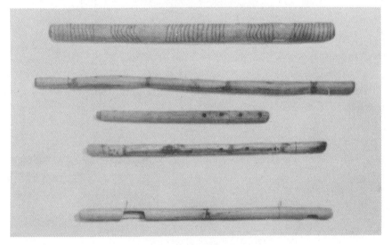

Plate 5: Washint

Plate 6: Embilta, washint, baganna and atamo

Plate 7: Massenqo and malakat

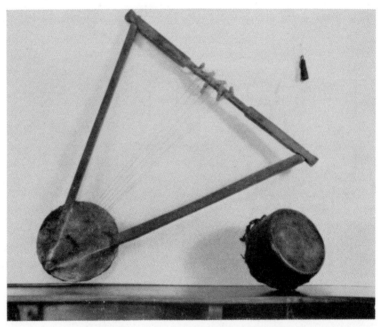

Plate 8: Qatchel, krar and atamo

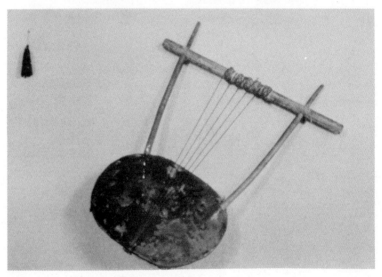

Plate 9: Krar and qatchel

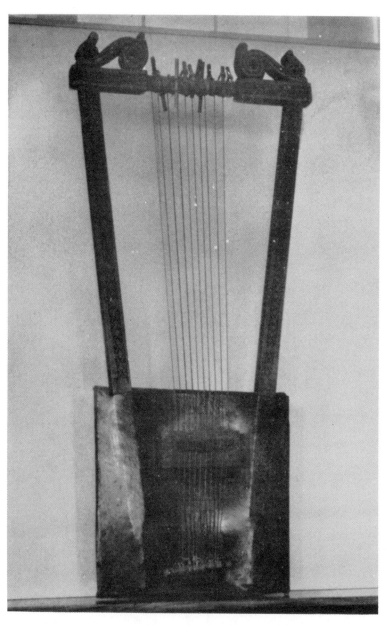

Plate 10: Baganna

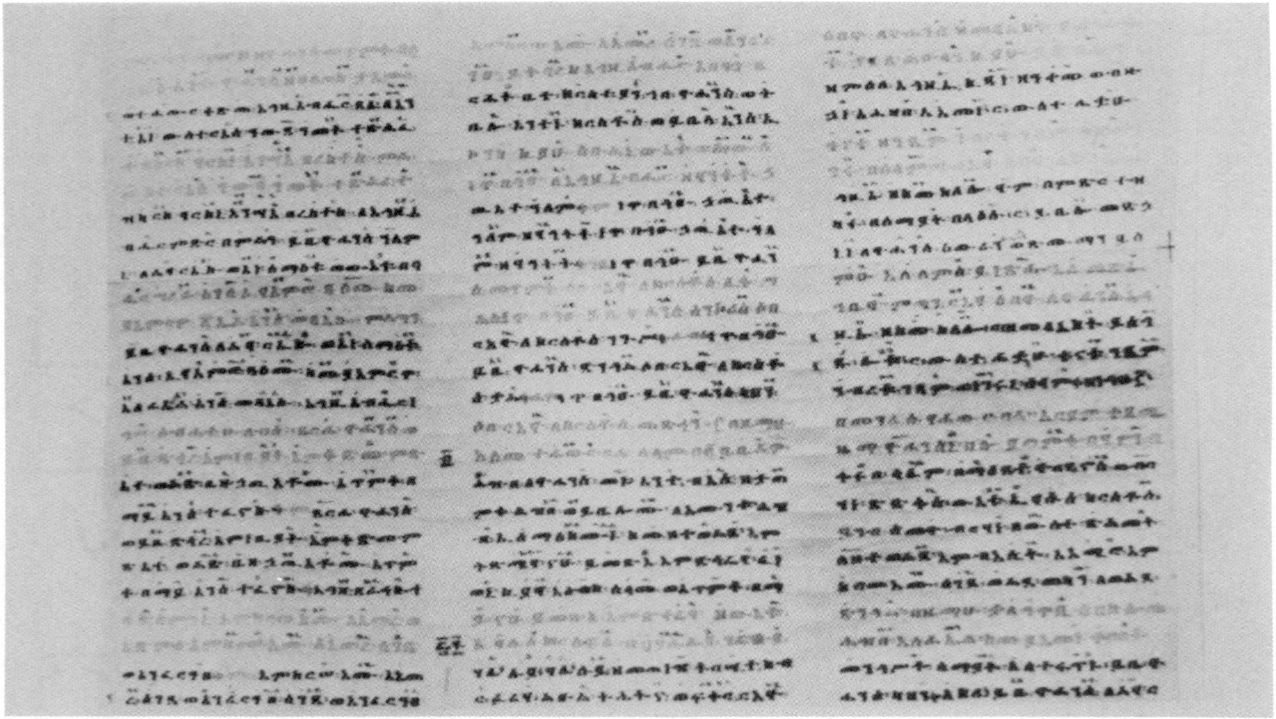

Plate 11: A page of ecclesiastical chant manuscript

or shell; the bamboo may be covered all over with leather or skin, which sometimes may be decorated with pricked or burnt patterns.

The two examples in the Museum, catalogue nos. 1541 and 832, are 105 cm. and 98 cm. long respectively. 1541 has a tin bell-mouth, and is decorated mainly with canvas wrapped round it and bound with ordinary wire. Near the mouthpiece end it is sheathed in a bright metal cylinder that on close inspection proves to be the discarded barrel of a pocket electric torch. Altogether it seems to be an inferior instrument. 832 has a bell-mouth made of gourd or wood, and is ornamented with a few thongs wound round the top, middle and end of the pipe.

1541 has a brass mouthpiece that looks as if it was taken from an ordinary European trumpet or other brass wind instrument. This mouthpiece, as well as the torch barrel, may be seen on the extreme right of Plate 7. 832 has no such additional mouthpiece, and the player has to exert a mighty lip pressure on the large open end of the bamboo in order to produce a trumpet-like sound.

According to Mondon-Vidailhet, on each malakat, 'not far from the mouthpiece there is a hole which gives a semi-tone above the highest note of the instrument'.[1] 1541 at the Museum does not have this finger-hole, although 832 does.

The malakat as described here is another ceremonial instrument, taking its place with the embilta and negarit as the 'insignia of royalty'. It was used to herald the approach of the king or a high nobleman. Malakats 'often preceded the king of kings in battle; I doubt whether they appear thus today'.[2] An example of a malakat fanfare is quoted from Mondon-Vidailhet at Ex. 7. He describes the instrument as having 'a beautiful military sound. The skill of the players consists of giving to these sounds a strident character and a strong military flavour. I know that they succeed in this, though the effects that can be produced are necessarily

---

[1] p. 3185.　　[2] Ibid.

very limited.'[1] Several malakats were amongst the orchestra of traditional instruments in the Silver Jubilee procession,[2] playing fanfares just like the one quoted from Mondon-Vidailhet. They did not seem to make use of the semitonal finger-hole, if indeed this was a feature of the instruments being used.

Ex. 7

The malakat, being an instrument that usually belonged to an important person, would earn respect even for a humble person fortunate enough to possess one. Marcel Griaule went on a hippopotamus-hunting expedition on Lake Tana, guided by some members of the Waito tribe. In this abbreviated extract from his story, he describes an event concerning a malakat-playing tribesman.[3]

One Waito had a trumpet in his belt. 'What are you going to do with that trumpet?' he was asked, when he still had one foot on land.

'Isn't the trumpet a sign of authority?' he answered, vexed, withdrawing his foot from the raft. Then he embarked on the raft and squatted, abusing his neighbours good-humouredly. 'Oh, ignorant! deaf!' he repeated.

As they neared their quarry, suddenly the owner of the trumpet declared with an oath that his trumpet had fallen into the water.

'Go on !' said the hunter.

'What? Abandon the trumpet?'

The hunter gave the men permission to dive for the instrument, and it was at once recovered and given back, full of water, to its owner. Without thanking them or emptying it he put it to his mouth and splashed a fine rain on his neighbours, belching rending sounds.

'To love the trumpet is to love you,' he added. 'The trumpet is authority. Who bears a trumpet on land? Leaders, great foreigners,

---

[1] p. 3185   See p. 15 above.
[3] *Abyssinian Journey,* trans. Rich (London, 1935), pp. 183–7.

and merchants of importance! Behind the trumpet wealth and honours abound!'

Figure 4 shows an instrument very similar to the highlands malakat. It comes from the Dime tribe, in the extreme south-west of Ethiopia. It is over 1·5 metres long, and is bound with leather. It has no finger-holes, but there is a wind-hole about 13 cm. from the mouthpiece.

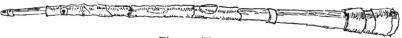

Fig. 4. Trumpet

(iv) In Plate 6 there is a long bamboo pipe (catalogue no. 1687) stretching diagonally across the display. There is also a long pipe running across the top. These are both funeral pipes from the Kambatta tribe. The upper one is about 2·1 metres long; the very long one extends to over 2·75 metres. At the lower end of the longer one a cow-horn is bound to the pipe with leather thongs. Neither instrument has any finger-holes. Both these are used to announce a death. It is the custom of this mostly-pagan tribe from the southern Rift Valley to use a long pipe for the death of a man, and a shorter pipe for the death of a woman, and these two are examples of such pipes.

As was the case with percussion instruments, earlier authorities mention types of wind instruments other than those described above. They are quoted here, chiefly from Mondon-Vidailhet,[1] in order to keep the record as nearly complete as possible. I did not find any information about them to corroborate or deny what is quoted here.

In his *Description de l'Egypte* Villoteau mentions instruments called *Zegouf, Ghenta,* and *Qand*. The first was a sort of flute resembling the Egyptian nay. The second was a horn which shepherds used to gather their flocks. Mondon-Vidailhet says 'these words are unknown today'. But he points to the possibility that 'certain of these instruments,

[1] p. 3186.

which I have not seen, are still used in some provinces. I ought to add that certain of their names belong to the liturgical language (Ge'ez or Ethiopic), which explains why one does not hear them spoken of today.'

His explanation of qand is that 'it is the generic name for horns. It means, properly speaking, "horns" or even "tusks". Elephant tusks served the Gallas for the manufacture of horns, which were called "Toultoulba", the name also given to the Turkish bugle.'

Tsegaye Gabre Medhin corrected this last name to 'toultoula', which is the name given to a bugle today in the army. Whichever way it is spelt, it is an interesting onomato-poetic word.

Villoteau also mentions the *T'aqa*, which Mondon-Vidailhet says is the common whistle, having heard no mention of it 'except as being used among the Gallas'.

Finally, Mondon-Vidailhet quotes his compatriot, La Borde, as speaking of an Ethiopian flute called the *Kwetz* or *Agada*, in his *Essai sur la musique*. According to this report, 'its shape and size are those of the German flute; but it is played like the "flûte à bec", with a mouthpiece like that of the clarinet. The sound is somewhat sharp, like that of the oboe, and does not rise very high; it would not be esteemed in the country if it was softer.'

Mondon-Vidailhet's comment is that 'agada' is an Amharic word meaning 'stalk of maize, hollow stem, shin-bone'. 'I do not recollect having heard it used for the flute. As for the word "kwetz", it is unknown to me, and Abyssinians to whom I have spoken of it also have been ignorant of it.'

(c) Stringed Instruments

(i) The *Massenqo* is a one-string fiddle, and is the only Ethiopian bowed instrument. It consists of a wooden body or sound box, sometimes square but more usually diamond-shaped in plan. This body is made of wild olive (qori). The face and back of the body are left open, but the sides are solid. The rounded or square length of wood that forms the neck is inserted through the middle of one corner of the body, and protrudes through the opposite corner for about 4 cm. or 5 cm. The face and back of the box are each covered in tanned cowhide or parchment, making a sounding board, and these skins extend right round and over the body, the edges being stitched together down the side of the box. The neck is sometimes decorated with burnt or carved patterns, and near the top has a peg or key used for tensioning the string.

The string almost always is of many strands of horsehair, making a string at least as thick as the lowest string of the European cello. Occasionally the string is literally a piece of string, very coarse-fibred. It passes from the tuning peg to the bridge.[1] The latter is shaped like a wide-splayed inverted 'V', sometimes being rounded more into a 'U' shape. The string passes through a hole at the apex of the bridge, the legs of which stand just above the centre of the sounding board. Immediately behind the bridge the string is knotted to the splayed fastener, of ordinary string or a leather thong, which leads on either side of the bottom corner of the sound box and is looped round the projecting bottom end of the neck-pole.

The bow is sharply arc-shaped and about 36 cm. long. It is more curved at the end opposite the hand-grip. The bow-string is of horsehair and is very thick.

The three examples of massenqo in the Museum may be seen in Plate 7, and their details are given here from the left (furthermost) instrument to the right. The bow of each

---

[1] The Amharic name for the bridge is *'faras'*, according to Mondon-Vidailhet, p. 3186. This word means 'horse', literally. The French for a violin bridge is 'chevalet' (from the root 'cheval'—horse). Speculation is interesting, but probably vain, on this terminological link.

instrument is hanging with the hand-grip at the bottom, in
this photo.

Catalogue No.	Overall length	String length peg-to-bridge	Sound-box size			Neck shape
			Diagonally width × height	Depth		
1756	79 cm.	46 cm.	22 cm. × 25 cm.	8 cm.		square
—	72 cm.	42 cm.	23 cm. × 27 cm.	12 cm.		square, decorated
—	77·5 cm.	44·5 cm.	28 cm. × 28 cm. (square)	13 cm.		round, with square section at top.

The massenqo players in the Orchestra said that five sound-
holes are always punched in the skin sounding board, one
at each corner and one exactly in the centre. None of the
three Museum instruments has this feature. Probably the
somewhat sophisticated Orchestra players have observed
that sound-holes improve their instruments, although this
feature is not to be found in the truly traditional pattern of
the massenqo.

The player of the massenqo is seated. He holds the
instrument between his knees, the back towards him and
the top of the neck resting against his left shoulder. The
fingers and thumb of the left hand are all used to stop the
string. The right hand is the bow-hand. The holding
stance is very like that for the smaller viol.

One would never imagine that the players could draw such resonances
from such a primitive instrument, but nevertheless some of them
possess real virtuosity. They make use of position-work and even
produce harmonics. What is even stranger is that they resort to the
vibrato, to bring variety into their melodies, in the same way as do our
violinists and cellists. As for the tablature, it approximates more to
the viola than to the violin or cello.[1]

---

[1] Mondon-Vidailhet, p. 3186.

The sound seems as though it is permanently muted, even when compared with that of a viol; but it is quite strident.

The massenqo is almost entirely a secular instrument, although a consort of massenqos may sometimes be found playing purely instrumental monophony before some big religious festival such as Maskal.[1] Most villages in the highlands have at least one massenqo player, but the instrument is typically associated with the *Azmari,*[2] or troubadour. Its usual role is that of accompanying songs, and there is a distinct genre of massenqo song, including all the typical themes of a troubadour or trouvère. It is also used in solo pieces, and in preludes or interludes that alternate with the verses of the songs. Both the solos and the songs are improvised as often as not. The Azmari slings his massenqo round his neck like a guitar when he is on the road, and this sling can be seen on the left-hand instrument in Plate 7.

Ethiopian culture never was a begetter of other cultures, even by remote influence, and in only a few instances is it the offspring. The massenqo is a case in point. It and the Arabian rebab are obviously blood-brothers, and it is probable that the Ethiopian instrument owes its origin to the Arabian. The rebab is probably the first bowed stringed instrument, and certainly the first known to us.[3] Through the rebab the massenqo can be linked with the European rebec, which name is a corruption of the Arabic name. However, the rebec, or rubebe, had two or even three strings, and is the direct ancestor of our Stradivarius. The Arabian and Ethiopian instruments have remained one-string fiddles to this day. In Europe, the custom of playing songs in unison with the voice, which came into vogue in the fifteenth century, led to the classification of rebecs into sets of treble, alto, tenor, and bass,[4] but in Ethiopia the

---

[1] See Chap. 4 (g). [2] See Chap. 3 (a) (i).
[3] *Grove,* Vol. VII, p. 2. [4] *Grove,* Vol. VII, p. 70.

instrument has never been developed in various sizes, playing at differing pitches.

Fr. Alvares, who went to Ethiopia in the sixteenth century, mentioned the massenqo in a curiously confused way.[1] 'There are . . . some instruments with chords [sic], square like harps, which they call David moçanquo (ya Dawit masanqo—fiddle of David, an instrument with one string) which means the harp of David. They play these to the Prester, and not well.' David's harp was a plucked instrument, not a one-string fiddle. How the confusion arose that is apparent in this quotation is not plain; but I think the reference may be taken as a clear indication of the existence of the one-string fiddle in Ethiopia at the time Alvares visited the country.

(ii) This and section (iii) which follows deal respectively with the *krar* and *baganna*, both plucked stringed instruments. They have much in common with the classical Greek lyre, as well as with each other, and so discussion of their relationship to other instruments is held over to section (iv).

The *Krar* is a six-stringed instrument, small enough to be held on the lap or against the hip. The body consists of a shallow circular bowl. Formerly this was hollowed out of a single piece of wood, but nowadays it is often merely an enamel plate. If made of wood, the underside of the bowl may or may not be cut off to give a flat bottom. Occasionally the sound-box, when made of wood, is box-like rather than bowl-like. Over the front or opening of the bowl a piece of roughly-made parchment is stretched by a wire threaded through holes in its edge and tightened under the lip of the bowl. A second piece of parchment covers the underside, in most cases, and is fastened to the wire with thongs. Pankhurst says there are four sound-holes in the parchment sounding-board,[2] but this is not always so.

Out of the bowl there protrude horizontally (when the bowl is held flat) the two arms of the instrument. These are

---

[1] *The Prester John of the Indies*, p. 516.　　[2] p. 412.

joined together where they are held against the inner rim
of the bowl, under the parchment, by a wire that loops over
to the tightening-wire beneath the outer lip. The arms are
splayed out at an angle from each other and emerge through
the parchment at points on the circumference diagonally
opposite where they are joined to each other and to the
bowl. The yoke which joins the bars at their top ends forms
a triangle with the bars, as Plate 8 shows.

The six gut strings are fastened at the bottom to a wire
loop which passes immediately above the base of the arms
and is fastened in its turn to the parchment-wire. They pass
over a shallow notched bridge that sits right in the centre
of the very taut parchment sounding-board, and thence
straight up to the centre section of the yoke. Here they are
wound round several times and held by pegs. These pegs
are not inserted into the wood as the pegs of a violin are
inserted into the neck; they work in much the same way as
a cross-bow saw is tensioned, and are held from slipping
by the pressure of the strings wound round them and round
the yoke in a special way. The part of the yoke where the
strings are wound is usually covered in leather or canvas.
According to Mondon-Vidailhet, 'normally the krar has
five or ten strings';[1] but the typical highlands krar today
definitely is six-stringed.

There are three krars in the Museum. Two of them are to
be seen in Plates 8 and 9. Details of their similarities and
points of variance are shown overleaf, listing the three in the
order in which they are displayed, from left to right. The
middle one comes from the Konso people, in Gemu Goffa
province on the southern plateau edges. Though its basic
concept is that of a highlands krar, it differs in more
respects than those revealed above. Its strings have no pegs
to tension them, but are only wound round the yoke
repeatedly. There is no bridge, and the strings are all tied
to one little stick, which is held tightly against the underlip

---

[1] p. 3187.

E   [45]

Position (in Museum display)	Left	Middle	Right
Plate No.	8	9	—
Catalogue No.	—	1196	—
Length of arms	76 cm.	54·5 cm.	66 cm.
Width of yoke	69 cm.	28 cm.	67 cm.
Diameter of bowl	22 cm.	29 × 22 cm. (oval)	18 cm.
Depth of bowl	7·5 cm.	4·5 cm.	4 cm.
Material of sound-box	Wooden bowl	Wooden bowl	Enamel dish
Shape of sound-box	Cut off flat on underside	Completely rounded	Plate-like
Position of bridge	Just below centre	No bridge	Very near top edge
No. of strings	6	5	6
Shape of arms	Square	Unshaped sticks	Crudely rounded

of the bowl by the strings stretched up to the yoke through a little hole in the lip of the bowl and the skin covering. The instrument is covered in a single piece of rough cowhide, laced tightly across the bottom of the bowl. The right-hand instrument comes from Wollega province, in the far west. It has a leather plectrum attached by a cord. As its yoke width is greater than the length of its arms, the latter are at a considerably wider angle than the arms on the first one, which has arms 8 cm. longer than the yoke width.

Figure 5 shows a five-stringed instrument of the Male people, in extreme south-west Ethiopia. It is about 90 cm. high. The body is made of a tortoise-shell covered with hide. Its size makes it closer to the baganna, but having only five strings it is more krar-like.

Fig. 5

If the player is seated, he holds the krar with one side resting along the top of his left thigh, so that the sound-box comes just under his left armpit, with the face of the instrument towards him, and the top projecting straight in front of him. The left arm comes over the upper edge of the body of the instrument, and the hand reaches out behind the instrument in such a way that the fingers and thumb can be used to damp the strings that should not sound, right up near the yoke. Sometimes the left-hand fingers pluck the strings, but in general this is the work of the right hand, which plucks the strings halfway between the bridge and the rim of the sound-box. Sometimes only the fingers are used; more often it is a plectrum, made of leather or the talon of some animal of prey, that is used. The plectrum is fastened to one of the arms of the instrument by a cord. There is also a cord stretched between the two arms in such a way that it passes over the player's left wrist and helps support the instrument. When played standing, the krar is held against the left hip, nearer to the horizontal than vertical, as is the case when the player is seated. The sound of the krar approximates to that of the viola played pizzicato, being quite rich in quality.

The krar plays an entirely secular role in Ethiopian music. It is a more popular instrument than the massenqo, being very much easier to play. Moreover, as mentioned already, the massenqo is in particular the instrument of the troubadours, 'who are no more esteemed than our jongleurs of the Middle Ages'. Therefore 'the krar is considered to be a nobler instrument'.[1]

Before the krar is tuned in any of its four different ways, the pitch has to be decided upon. If it is accompanying a singer on its own, the strings are tuned to suit his or her voice-range. If, however, a washint is being used as well, the washint player selects an instrument suited to the singer's voice and the range of the song, and the krar is tuned to that washint.

The four different tuning systems are each known by a name which originated from some tribe or region. The names have now lost any geographical significance they had. Thus any tuning can be used to play music from any region, and none is kept solely for one type of music. The krar can be tuned to any size of washint, big or small, in any of the four ways.

In this explanation of the systems, the notes of the washint are given the same arbitrary names as before, that is, A–C–D–E–G, ascending from the note played with all four finger-holes stopped. The strings are listed from 1 to 6, No. 1 being the right-hand string on the instrument in Plate 8, or the lowest string when the instrument is on its side in the playing-stance. This string is the first one to be tuned, and may be considered as the tonal centre in each case.

------

[1] Mondon-Vidailhet, p. 3188.

First, the *tizita* tuning, tuned to the washint's second note, C.
The krar's notes are:

I	2	3	4	5	6
c'	c	ab	g	eb	db

Second, the *ba'ati* tuning, to the washint's A, or lowest note:

I	2	3	4	5	6
a'	a	g	e	d	c

Third, the *ambassal* tuning, pitched to the washint's top note, G:

I	2	3	4	5	6
g'	g	eb'	d'	c'	ab

Fourth, the *anchihoye* system, tuned to the note played by the washint with the lowest and second-lowest holes open, that is, D (additionally sharpened above its always slightly sharp pitch, because when the anchihoye system is in use the washint player always opens these two holes together to produce his third note).

I	2	3	4	5	6
		♯	♯		
d'	d	b	g	g	eb

(The sharp placed above the note means it is very slightly sharpened, but not so much as a quarter-tone, in relation to the tonal centre (string I).)

It is to be observed that the tizita and ambassal tunings are almost identical, the only difference being that the fifth string is tuned a major 6th below the tonal centre in tizita, while in ambassal it is a 5th below. The first three tunings are entirely comprehensible and acceptable to western ears and it is only the anchihoye tuning that strikes us as really strange. In this case, not only is the tuning of the krar remarkable: the tonal centre is the one note (D) of the washint that is to western ears slightly out of tune, and

[49]

this means that emphasis is constantly being laid on an out-of-tune centre. It must not be forgotten, incidentally, that this 'out-of-tune' judgement is a purely subjective European concept, which would never occur to an Ethiopian.

As far as the washint is concerned, when the tizita tuning is being used the scale is only a four-note one, for the lowest note of the washint (A) is never used with this tuning.

'Ethiopian music is largely pentatonic' is a common conception; but it is a generalized kind of inaccuracy, perpetuated, by implication, even in *Grove*, in remarks based on the tuning of the krar. In the article on the lyre, the firm suggestion is made that the tuning of the Ethiopian lyre, or krar, first quoted by Villoteau in 1799 as D'–G–A'–B'–E', is 'a possible reminiscence of ancient Greece. This tuning is the probable tuning of the old 5-string Greek lyre.'[1] Curt Sachs says that 'all lyres of which we know the tuning, in ancient Greece as well as in modern Nubia and Ethiopia, have been submitted to the usual pentatonic genus with minor 3rds, that is, E–G–A–B–D continued upwards and downwards according to the number of strings'.[2] It is true that the washint usually plays a pentatonic series of notes, and that the washint and krar hold the key place in secular music. But it must be strongly denied that krar music is pentatonic to any great extent. In the first place, there is the existence of the quadritonic tizita scale already mentioned. Secondly, the interval of a semitone does not occur in the pentatonic scale; yet in three of the four krar tuning systems there is a semitone—in tizita, between the third and fourth strings, and second and sixth; the same in ambassal; and in anchihoye between the second

[1] Vol. V, pp. 453ff.
[2] *The Rise of Music in the Ancient World East and West* (New York, 1943), p. 72. So long as the krar is in fact related to the five-string lyre, Sachs' last remark here is a reasonable explanation of why the krar's sixth string echoes the note of the fifth string at an octave distant.

and sixth strings.[1] This fact at once reduces the likelihood, in many cases, of krar music being pentatonic.

Thirdly, when the krar and washint play together, sometimes the latter plays the melody and the former adds its own embellishment. (Sometimes the krar only plays chord accompaniments.) If all the notes that can be played by the krar and/or the washint in any tuning system are written out as one scale, as has been done in Exx. 8–11, it will be found that these same three tunings, tizita, ambassal, and anchihoye, are very far removed indeed from the plain pentatonic scale.[2]

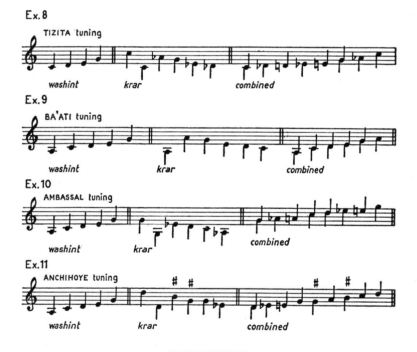

Ex. 8

TIZITA tuning

washint   krar   combined

Ex. 9

BA'ATI tuning

washint   krar   combined

Ex. 10

AMBASSAL tuning

washint   krar   combined

Ex. 11

ANCHIHOYE tuning

washint   krar   combined

---

[1] In anchihoye there is additionally the microtonal interval between the fourth and fifth strings.

[2] The challenge presented here to the pentatonic notion about Ethiopian music is only concerned with secular music. Much of the flavour of Ethiopian church music is definitely pentatonic.

On the other hand, the ba'ati tuning clearly is pentatonic, both when the krar alone is considered and when the krar and washint scales are combined.

A possible reason for the lowest washint note not being used with the tizita krar tuning is that, if it were introduced, it would give a scale of nine notes within the 'octave'. As it is, both tizita and ambassal keep to an octave of eight notes, although anchihoye has nine (only eight if the microtonic interval between the fourth and fifth notes of the consolidated scale is ignored), and ba'ati is pentatonic as already stated.

It does not seem possible to rationalize these four tuning systems, and the main purpose of this discussion has been to show that it is misleading to think of Ethiopian secular music as being to any marked extent based on the pentatonic scale.

This complex tuning system was explained and demonstrated to me by the leading krar player of the Orchestra. It was verified by authorities in Ethiopia that the origin of the system has been forgotten, but that it dates from a long time ago. So far as I know, the system has not been recorded before, all earlier writers having based their ideas on the pentatonic tuning of the krar given by Villoteau, who never even set foot in Ethiopia but worked on material supplied by Ethiopian priests and monks whom he met in Egypt. Perhaps the more austere ba'ati tuning was the only one the churchmen would be willing to recognize, putting aside the more worldly and resourceful other tunings. Notably, *Grove* bases its remarks on this authority from 150 years ago. Mondon-Vidailhet is the only writer even to make a suggestion of the existence of other tuning systems. This is in his section on the baganna, another stringed instrument closely related to the krar.

I have tried, without success, to ascertain the manner in which this instrument is tuned. I have had to give it up, inasmuch as it has variations, resulting perhaps from the fact that the bagannas are not

tuned, or perhaps that there are certain differences in the tuning of the
instrument, according to the songs that it has to accompany.[1]

Villoteau has a lengthy discussion as to why the Ethiopians used the krar tuning method that he gave (D'–G–A'–
B'–E'). In this note series he saw the harmonic progression
set out in Ex. 12, which he links directly with the Greek
tuning system.

Ex.12

In supposing that this tuning resulted from an ancient musical system
(for it has no such appearance as to make it a derivative from modern
music), how is it, we may ask ourselves, that early musicians introduced
fifths in it? They only thought of such tuning as indirect or inverted
harmony, and allowed fifths neither in the harmonic foundation of
their music nor in the tuning of any of their instruments. . . . But, the
fifth being an inversion of the fourth, it is only necessary to invert it,
that is to say to substitute for the sharp sound a more serious sound, in
order to rediscover this fourth, and it is the ordinary method that old
musicians used in making the score for their stringed instruments; it
is also the method followed by the Arabs; equally it is what we follow,
in an opposite sense; it consists of rising to the octave above the tuned
pitch and tuning this octave with the preceding note. By this means
the note which would have made the sharp-sounding fifth forms the
fourth with the serious-sounding octave of this same sharp sound, and
this inversion allows them to avoid sounding the fifth. The Arabs
use no other method of tuning their instruments, and it is probable
that it is thus that the Ethiopians have arrived at fixing the pitch of
the strings of their krar.[2] Without doubt they have also had an
instrument which served as a guide, that is to say their canon, with
which they have fixed with precision the harmonic relation of the
tuned pitches of this lyre; and since they have been fixed, here is how

---

[1] p. 3188.
[2] Villoteau in fact refers repeatedly to the *kissar*, a name which is non-
existent in Ethiopia and which Mondon-Vidailhet says should be 'krar'.

they have had to arrange the strings and their pitches, in order to avoid the fifth (see Ex. 13). One sees that, by this method of arranging

Ex. 13

the tuning of the krar, following the method of the Greeks, which is also that of the Arabs, there are no fifths, but only fourths and octaves.

Villoteau continues with a long explanation of the relationship of this tuning with the Greek system. He says that each of the fourths shown in Ex. 13 corresponds to one of the principal tetrachords of the system perfected by the Greeks. Expressed in manuscript, these tetrachords give the series of sounds shown in Ex. 14 (a). Ex. 14 (b) shows what

Ex. 14

would happen if the fourth above the last note were added, introducing the third flat, and giving five series each of four notes.

And in continuing thus, each new tetrachord, that is to say each new series of notes, would give a further flat, which will present, in the order shown here, the principles of the musical systems of all peoples. Thus it is apparent that neither chance nor caprice determined the choice of notes in the tuning of the krar, because they show themselves to be directly derived from the fundamental principle of harmony, whether ancient or modern.[1]

Remembering the date when Villoteau was writing, we need not take his generalization 'of all peoples' too seriously. The whole passage seems to be labouring hard to prove a

---

[1] For the full extract, see Mondon-Vidailhet, pp. 3187–8.

preconceived notion. He does not offer any explanation about why the strings are arranged in the inverted order that they are.

(iii) The *Baganna* is a considerably larger ten-stringed lyre. In all major respects the construction is like that of the krar, but there are minor points of dissimilarity. The body of the baganna usually is shaped like a section cut out of a pyramid. Some examples have a section of a cone as their sound-box, so modified that the face of the instrument is roughly square. In both cases the larger section is the face of the body, which tapers off to the narrower section at the back. The instrument occasionally has a bowl-shaped body, like the typical krar. The body is entirely covered in skin or parchment, of much better quality than the krar skin. Stretched over the open front of the body, the skin forms the sounding-board, and is neatly stitched down the corners of the sides of the body. In most examples there is a rectangular sound-hole roughly in the middle of the sounding-board. This may be hidden beneath the wide bridge.

The two arms are fixed to the lower edge of the front of the sound-box, under the parchment, about one-third of the way from each bottom corner. They project from under the parchment, in the same plane as the front of the instrument, at a much less acute angle to each other than do the krar arms, and are joined by a yoke at the top. The overall shape of the baganna is almost rectangular, noticeably contrasting with the triangular shape of the krar.

The ten gut strings that are a standard feature of the baganna[1] are fastened to the yoke as the krar strings are, and pass from the middle of the yoke (which is wrapped in leather or cloth, as is the krar's) down to a generously-proportioned bridge. This stands, in most cases, about one-quarter of the way between the top and bottom edges of the sounding-board, though it may be much nearer the bottom

---

[1] Pankhurst says it has eight, p. 410.

than top. It is between 4 and 5 cm. high, it is about
13 cm. wide, and made of a broad piece of wood fastened
at each end to a piece at right-angles; thus it stands up
square from the sounding-board, in contrast to the arched
shape of the massenqo bridge and the shallow shape
of the krar bridge. Each string rests in a little U-shaped
piece of leather. From the bridge the strings pass to a
wooden rod on to which they are all tied. This rod is just
above the lower edge of the sound-box, and is fastened by
two leather thongs to the underside of the box.

There are four typical bagannas in the Museum. The
second one in the list that follows may be seen in Plate 10;
the fourth one is the furthermost instrument in Plate 6.

Catalogue No.	Height	Width at yoke	Sounding-board width × height	Shape of body	Depth of body	Position of bridge
—	119 cm.	57 cm.	38 × 37 cm.	pyramid-section	23 cm.	above centre
922	105 cm.	49·5 cm.	37 × 38 cm.	pyramid-section	23 cm.	above centre
535	109 cm.	48 cm.	41 × 34 cm.	conical section	20 cm.	above centre
—	99 cm.	43 cm.	33 × 33 cm.	pyramid-section	30·5 cm.	below centre

In Plate 6, the nearer stringed instrument (catalogue
no. 197), which comes from the Konso people in the far
south of the country, seems to be a cross between a baganna
and a krar. Its size, and the fact that its arms are not splayed
out to any noticeable degree, make it like the baganna; but
it only has five strings. Its overall height is 76 cm.; the
width at the yoke is 37 cm.; the front of the sound-box
measures 28 × 36 cm. The body is simply made, being a
hollowed-out section of tree-trunk with one side sliced right

off. The bottom, back and sides of the curved body are solid; the front and top are open. The whole is covered in roughly-cured cowhide. The body is 30·5 cm. deep, and stands 51 cm. high at the back. There is no bridge, and the strings all pass through one hole in the hide near the bottom edge of the sounding-board. In this respect this Konso baganna is like the Konso krar described above and shown in Plate 9. The most striking feature of the Konso baganna is the way in which the arms arch out sharply from the plane of the front of the body, in a fashion not to be seen in the highlands baganna or in the krar. The Curator suggested that it is possible that all Konso instruments, whether as large as the baganna or smaller like the krar, have only five strings.

As the baganna is so tall, the player rests it on the floor beside his chair and holds it upright. His right hand plucks the strings, which face towards his left side, and a plectrum is almost always used. His left hand is behind the instrument, stopping the strings. It is interesting that, according to Pankhurst, the Amharic phrase for playing the baganna is literally translated into English as 'to strike' the baganna. The word 'plectrum' derives from the Greek 'plektron, plessein, to strike', and so we find that the Ethiopians use a verb that in meaning corresponds exactly to the Greek root, even though they call the striking-implement by a quite different word ('mametcha' or 'tchera match').[1]

The baganna produces serious-sounding notes and is generally thought of as a dignified instrument. It was the only instrument that persons of the highest dignity would stoop to learn, and it has come to be thought of as the perquisite only of the Emperor and noblemen. Certainly it is made with rather more care than is the average Ethiopian musical instrument. The arms and yoke have a heavier burden of carved ornamentation, the skin is better treated, and the woodwork stained a more sober colour, than one would find in other instruments. Perhaps the instrument

---

[1] Pankhurst, p. 410 and footnote; Mondon-Vidailhet, p. 3187.

has been reserved for royalty because of its strong associations with the harp of David.[1] However, players of lower rank are to be found. The music played on the baganna is always rather solemn. It is used particularly during Lent, accompanying songs with a definitely sacred emphasis; but it would not be correct to name the baganna as an instrument of the church—it is only played outside the church, in the home. Because of its association with only one type of music, it is not used in an ensemble of instruments. 'In general, the baganna songs are true cantilenas, somewhat long-winded works.'

Mondon-Vidailhet gives the tuning system as found in Villoteau, and this system appears to be the one used even today for the baganna's limited range of music. It is D–B'–E'–D'–G–A'–E–G,–A–B. The former authority says that the four middle strings in pitch (i.e. D', G, A', E) are called 'boz', which means 'fools'—probably being so called 'because they reproduce notes given by the other strings'.[2] This tuning is not varied, as is the krar tuning. It is pentatonic.

(iv) The differences between the baganna and krar are of no importance when considering the relationship between the Ethiopian plucked instruments and some instruments of other countries and civilizations, for their basic similarities are close enough to make it plain they have a common origin. It is convenient, therefore, to call them by the one name, the Ethiopian lyre; bearing in mind that the Ethiopian lyre has been variously recorded as having three,[3] five, six, eight, or even ten strings.

The Ethiopian lyre has obvious similarities with various Egyptian, Greek, and European instruments.[4] The early Egyptian lyre and the Egyptian kithara have in common with the baganna a square or rectangular body. This points

---

[1] See section (c) (iv) of this chapter.   [2] p. 3189.
[3] See section (c) (v) of this chapter.
[4] The material in the remainder of this section is based on *Grove*, Vol. V, p. 453ff; Mondon-Vidailhet sections vii and viii; and the *Harvard Dictionary of Music*, especially under 'guitar'.

to a connection with the Greek kithara, a more sophisticated instrument than the Egyptian. A further line of similarity may be traced between the early Greek lyre and the Ethiopian lyre. Both have angled arms rising from the body. The body of the Greek instrument has a front shaped like a rectangle with the corners rounded off; this is an affinity with the rectangular-faced baganna sound-box, and the circular krar box.

Mondon-Vidailhet says the Ethiopian name 'krar' is derived from 'cither' or 'kithera'.[1] This gives a clear etymological link with the guitar family, which is of Oriental origin. The lute is a member of this family. The rounded back of its sound-box is an interesting feature shared with many Ethiopian lyres (especially the krar, but also the baganna at times).

Thus through name affinity we find the Ethiopian lyre is linked with the lute (through krar/guitar); yet in looks the Ethiopian lyre has all the appearances of a true lyre.

Mondon-Vidailhet thinks the Ethiopian lyre is 'borrowed from the Greeks'. It seems to me that he is wrong. The relation between the Greek and Ethiopian lyres is not along the vertical father-son line of a family tree, but more probably the horizontal brother-brother line, stemming from the same parent, the Egyptian lyre. There is very little evidence of any north-to-south cultural influence between Greece and Ethiopia, except through the Church after Ethiopia had been christianized in the fourth century. But there is incontrovertible evidence that whatever part of Ethiopian culture is derivative comes, with very few exceptions, from the country's immediate neighbours to the north-east and north, in Arabia and Egypt, over a period of many centuries.

Grove says that 'the lyre still played in Arabia and Ethiopia bears striking resemblance to the ancient lyre of the Greeks', but makes no suggestion as to the ancestry of

---

[1] Mondon-Vidailhet, p. 3186.

the Ethiopian instrument. The idea that both it and the Greek lyre may be of common descent is supported by a passage from Pankhurst (p. 409), unfortunately without references. There it is stated that the Ethiopian baganna 'resembles the lyre of the Greeks and Romans, which is considered by scholars to have originated in Asia, whence the Ethiopian people came, and whence they derived their ancient culture'.

It is very commonly said in Ethiopia that the Ethiopian lyre, especially in its baganna form, is exactly like 'the legendary harp which David used to calm the hypochondriacal attacks of Saul', in Mondon-Vidailhet's words. This he disputes. He thinks that 'the harp of the ancient Egyptians hardly resembled the Ethiopian lyre. It approximated more to our harp.' Such a harp had a cylindrical sounding-box, with a single arm that curves on out of one end of the cylinder, the strings being stretched from the arm back to the top side of the cylinder. The Egyptian harp was probably not so primitive, but basically the same. Mondon-Vidailhet thinks that David would have used this type of harp, and that it is unreasonable for the Ethiopians to claim that their baganna stems from his harp, seeing that the baganna is definitely of the lyre family, not the harp family.

Against this, we must set *Grove*'s opinion, where, after a description of the common chracteristics of the lyre family, we find that 'the *kinnor*, the national instrument of the ancient Jews, and that upon which David played before Saul, was a lyre of this type'. It was held with the strings almost horizontal, and played with a long thin plectrum. The yoke was curved or oblique, and there were between six and twelve strings. It is wrongly translated as 'harp' in the English Bible. Pointing out that the Ethiopian lyre is played either with a plectrum or with the fingers, *Grove* says that this recalls 'the passage in 1 Samuel xvi. 23, where David plays to Saul on the kinnor "with his hand" '.

If *Grove* is right, so are the Ethiopians. Then, if both the Ethiopian and the English Bibles used for David's instrument the name 'lyre', not 'harp', it could correctly be maintained that in the baganna there is a sure relic of biblical times. Of course, if Mondon-Vidailhet is right, the Ethiopian claim is wrong. On balance it seems preferable to support the Ethiopian belief. But to establish it beyond doubt would entail a long and arduous investigation of the development of plucked string instruments, in Arabia, Egypt, Greece, and Ethiopia, through a period of perhaps 2,500 years or more.

(v) The *'Enzira* probably was a rudimentary lyre. Villoteau[1] described it thus:

It is made with much less care than the baganna. The sounding box is also square, but it is less deep than that of the baganna. The crosspiece fitted to the two uprights is not absolutely horizontal; it is higher in the middle than at the sides; it even seems that the highest point is reached at a very open angle, and it is to this part of the crosspiece that the strings are attached.

Mondon-Vidailhet considered it plain that, with its three strings, 'this is only an elementary krar, used by the ordinary people'.[2] The curved yoke mentioned by Villoteau is an interesting link with the angled yokes of the Egyptian kithara and lyre. The word ' 'enzira' is Ethiopic for 'harp' or 'lyre'. It is possible that primitive forms of the Ethiopian lyre are still to be found in remote areas, but I was not able to find any information about an instrument under this name.

(vi) The idea of an instrumental consort is unknown in traditional secular music in Ethiopia. It would be seldom that more than a single drum was used to accompany a dance; krar-songs, baganna-songs or massenqo-songs would only have a single instrument accompanying them, even if a chorus joined in the singing. One might find a number of azmaris[3] or troubadours playing their massenqos in unison, but this would not be often, as so much of their music is improvised.

[1] op. cit.   [2] p. 3189.   [3] See Chap. 3 (a) (i).

The National Folklore Orchestra at the Haile Selassie I Theatre in the capital is an orchestra of folklore instruments. They play as a consort because of the size of the vast theatre which is their home, and the folk-songs and dances that are staged there are performed by as many as twenty dancers, a chorus, and the orchestra of ten or twelve players. In this respect they are cutting across tradition; but they are doing so in order to preserve it. Presenting folk music as they do, with a good deal of what is usually called 'showmanship', they attract good audiences, which probably they would not do if they were merely performing as the music and dances are performed in every village on the plateau. But the actual music, and the actual words of the songs, are all strictly folk-art. The dresses they wear are often reproductions of dresses and clothes that were once a part of Ethiopian ceremonial or daily life, but which now are rapidly fading into disuse.

When the orchestra is tuning up for a concert, all the players take their note from the washint, which plays the tuning note of the particular tuning-system that the krars are to follow. This tuning note is always the last note of the piece, and could well be called the tonal centre.

The orchestra does not have any bagannas. However, they need to have a lower-pitched sound than the krars and massenqos play, so they use an instrument that has been made as a cross between the krar and the baganna. It is not so large as the latter, which is unwieldy, and it has only six strings. This means it is tuned just as the krar is; but it must be emphasized that this tuning system is not used for a real baganna.

When I last saw the orchestra, in 1963, its forces consisted of 1 washint (the leader), 3 massenqos, 3 krars, 2 bass-krars, and 1 drummer. This last had 1 big kabaro and up to 7 other drums of various sizes. There was no conductor. Some of the songs they perform are solo songs, with only one instrument for the accompaniment, and there are also instrumental solos.

3 Secular Song and Dance

(a) Minstrels

(i) The *Azmari* is 'the singing gazelle of Ethiopia', a remarkable feature of the musical scene in the traditional highlands, but he is fast disappearing as the twentieth century ever reduces the demands for his skill. When Mondon-Vidailhet was in Ethiopia the azmari was still in his hey-day, which probably had lasted for many centuries.[1]

The Azmaris form one of the most extraordinary brotherhoods in Ethiopia, whose institutions have much in common with those of our Middle Ages, so that one might believe them to be descended therefrom. In the midst of barbarous Mohammedism, Abyssinia has cherished its bizarre Middle Ages aspect, and the azmaris are not the least of the features of resemblance. In effect they represent our troubadours or trouvères with astonishing fidelity. Wandering singers in the service of the princes and nobility, they come armed with their viols (the massenqo), improvident friends of pleasure, living on their caustic or gay spirits, as children of the household—but sometimes as 'enfants terribles'. Their pointed tongues do not always spare the great lord of the manor who feeds them, especially when they consider that the gifts they receive are not fit for their devil-may-care zest. . . . They are at all the feasts, and share with the clergy the least overestimated reputation of parasites.[2] Like the cricket, they sing all the summer, and I would not be surprised in the least if their improvidence leads them to a hard winter.

---

[1] Unacknowledged extracts in this section all come from Mondon-Vidailhet pp. 3182–3, or Pankhurst, p. 422ff.
[2] This is a reference to the fact that as much as one-third of the whole population of Ethiopia has been estimated to be priests or monks.

The parallel between the azmari and the troubadour of
France could be extended to include the minstrel who
wandered through England, the Celtic bard, the minne-
singers of Germany and the rhapsodes of ancient Greece.
Just as in Europe such minstrels often were in the employ
of kings and princes, so we find that in Ethiopia the
Emperor, as well as each nobleman, would have one or
more azmaris in his entourage. Again, just as the medieval
minstrel was not solely a court retainer, but also was a
wanderer, so we find from Pankhurst that 'itinerant azmaris
who accompanied the caravan and enlivened the journey with
songs of love and patriotism were numerous until recent
days. The great increase in motor transport has reduced
this branch of their activity, but strolling minstrels, passing
from farm to farm, have still their function and receive a
hospitable welcome and good cheer.'

The azmari first and foremost is an improviser. His
themes suit the occasion—but not always in the most
auspicious manner. He sings wedding songs, eulogies of
the virtues of the master of the house or of the beauties of
the lady, and epics of victories in war or conquests in love.
C. H. Rey visited the court of Ras Hailu, King of Gojjam
(in the early 1930s, before Gojjam was finally reduced to
the status of a province), and was entertained at a banquet.[1]

To complete the medieval effect, stray minstrels dotted about the hall
sang songs of praise to the donor of the feast and his ancestors, accompanying themselves on weird instruments consisting of a single string
stretched along a handle over a sheepskin-covered hollow frame.

With the histrionic sense inborn in every Ethiopian, the
azmari abruptly turns from praise to mockery and even
attack. By such means he attracts the more attention to
himself. But he must match the benefits of his scurrility
with its dangers. An increased measure of largesse from his
delighted hearers might be quite cancelled by the wrath of

[1] *The Real Abyssinia*, p. 111.

his principal benefactor, against whom the attacks are directed.

It even happens sometimes that, in spite of the kind of inviolacy that they enjoy, similar to that which grew round Voltaire, some revengeful stick crashes down at dusk on their emaciated backs. These are the little inconveniences of a profession which equally has some little advantages—not to scorn them too much—as has always been the case with the actor's profession in the houses of the great.

Another visitor to Ras Hailu's court found a vitriolic attack being delivered by an azmari. This was Marcel Griaule,[1] who went there in 1931. This azmari he describes as a hermaphrodite, who shouted his insults rather than singing them, although he was accompanied on the massenqo by a fellow-azmari. The attack ranged far and wide.

The hermaphrodite grasped the lateral folds of his robe; then, feet motionless, head and body turning right and left, knees stiff and bending regularly, the right hand at times free and carried to his ear as a gesture of suffering, tragic, eyes closed, vehement, he shouted at all and to the Prince magnificent insults.
The prince who dies yesterday, ah ! ah ! what sort of a man !
Master of a lousy dog and a diseased slave,
Master of a narrow footstool that he calls the royal bed. . . .
For a long time he continued a caricature of the Prince; the soldiers and the servants were delighted and alarmed. He took up everything: the management of the domanial property, the tax on coffee, the master's fear of seeing himself dispossessed by the eldest son, the haste he had used in proclaiming as heir his last-born, Yohannes, a turbulent child whose brain was nothing remarkable. He exposed in detail the politics of the campaign for prestige in this most miserable country, infested by land-hogs which disinter putrefying corpses by night, a country of weak churls with no shelter, where the dogs are leaner than anywhere else. He enumerated the storehouses, which should crack under the weight of the corn gathered as tax.
Zara-Brouk, granary one—empty !
Zara-Brouk, granary two—empty !
Zara-Brouk, granary three—empty !

[1] *Abyssinian Journey*, pp. 106ff.

His companion, his eyes on the body of his violin, beat his feet in time and hummed a tune through set jaws. From the string which he played with a small horse-hair bow he drew sounds which would make the cheek muscles in the most insensitive brute throb.

> The soldiers of the English consul
> Cannot eat red peppers.
> The soldiers of the German consul
> Cannot eat red peppers.
> The soldiers of a consul named Griaule
> Bravely press back against the wall when the hyena passes,
> And are such magicians
> That in order to bring back a belch that has escaped too quickly
> They suddenly grasp the shaming mouth !

The azmari continued with some terrible story from the past, and abruptly changed to verses about women in love. Every now and then he would utter some abject phrases or excuses, with deep reverences and closed eyes.

> Pardon, O my mare ! I owe you many debts !
> My body ! Oh ! My body !
> O slayer of my body !

A sudden effort of his whole person brought the hermaphrodite to his feet. While his companion, bewildered by fatigue, stamped his feet ecstatically, he again took up the abusive theme he had abandoned.

> Governor of the country of the Nile, you, rest on your laurels !
> The other one, the nephew of Menelik, Tafari[1] with the beautiful hands,
> Is spreading himself on the throne of the Queen of Sheba,
> While you, you sleep soundly,
> Stuck to your royal bed like a burnt girdle-cake !
> My body ! Oh ! My body !
> O slayer of my body !

What Griaule recorded in 1931 another traveller had seen more than 150 years earlier. James Bruce was in Ethiopia in the 1770s, and saw how these azmaris could

---

[1] A reference to Haile Selassie I, surnamed Tafari, who eventually brought Gojjam, and Ras Hailu, under the authority of the Imperial government.

[66]

easily give fatal offence with their tongues and their twisted songs.[1]

There were at Gondar a set of mummers, who were a mixture of buffoons and ballad singers. These people on all public occasions run about the streets, dancing, singing songs of their own composition, and performing all kinds of antics. Many a time, on his return from the field of victory, they had met Ras Michael and received his bounty for singing his praises. On the day when the Abuna (Archbishop) excommunicated the Ras, however, this set of vagrants had made part of the ceremony; they ridiculed and abused Michael, in scurrilous rhymes and songs, calling him crooked, lame, old and impotent. These wretches now met the Ras with songs of a different strain, welcoming him back to Gondar (after the Abuna had been overthrown) as they had in old times. Michael made a sign to the horse who were behind him to the number of 200; and they at once fell upon the singers. In less than two minutes they were all laid dead upon the field, except for one young man, mortally wounded.

Several months later, Bruce records, Ras Michael's horse twice threw him to the ground when he was riding on the very same smooth spot where these azmaris had suffered their unmusicianly death. 'Everyone interpreted these accidents as an omen that Michael's power and fortune were gone from him for ever. I could not help reflecting how justly the Ras was punished for the murder of the singers in that very place.'

Amharic, the national language of Ethiopia, is a flexible tongue. Scholars say that, moulded by a quick brain and an agile tongue, it is capable of as expressive, subtle, dramatic or forceful use as the great European languages. The azmari improvises in Amharic, often twisting words to suit his purpose in the most fanciful and far-fetched puns, most of which are quite untranslatable; for they depend for their outrageous effect upon the merest change of inflection that a foreigner would find it hard to detect. Sometimes he might

---

[1] *Bruce's Travels and Adventures in Abyssinia*, ed. Clingan (Edinburgh, 1860), pp. 256 and 269.

fit his improvisations to known traditional tunes, but more often he would improvise the music as well, adding on his massenqo 'some interesting preludes, which show a degree of virtuosity the more remarkable seeing that the instrument hardly lends itself to such performances, with its single string and its rudimentary structure.' Figurative usages abound in the language, the metaphors often reaching a degree of complexity where even the Ethiopian would find it difficult to explain the meaning, though he senses it clearly enough. Pankhurst gives some simple examples of azmari songs. In the one quoted here, an azmari was singing of the patriots' efforts to rehabilitate their country ('to make the house', the traditional circular house, with one central roof pillar) while it was subjugated by the Italians; but the Emperor was in exile.

> Ras Abeba Aragai ordered his patriots to make the house;
> Dedjazmatch Tashome did likewise;
> Falleke Lidj Ayhu did likewise;
> And also the proud Garasu did likewise;
> And the hero Kafallou did likewise;
> And all other heroes did likewise.

Name after name would be added, and after each line the hearers might well join in with a repeated 'ha !' or 'o-ho !' And after the names had accumulated there would come the point of the song:

> But the pillar had disappeared,
> Therefore the house could not be built.

The profession of azmari is not exclusive to men, and women troubadours attain the same level of skill in singing, playing, extemporizing, praising, and insulting as do the men. Mondon-Vidailhet writes of one who was renowned in his time. 'She played many instruments, but the one that was most appreciated "n'était peut-être pas celui qui sert à l'accompagnement ordinaire des azmari".'

The style of singing of the azmari is dramatic, demanding

the attention and arousing the enthusiasm of the listeners. 'He throws off vocal brilliancies, throat feats, coups de gorge, in the style of Arab singers, and these flourishes are intermingled with a kind of rapid recitative. It is here in particular that the words with double meanings and the formidable puns are given free rein. Every now and then the voice of the azmari pauses and he introduces a new verse with a little viol music. In fact, we see that, like our trouvères or jongleurs in the Middle Ages, the azmaris are as much musician as poet. Even the name that they bear means "singers" in Amharic.'

Of course, the azmaris do not perform just for the love of music. In court they expect their food and keep, and generous largesse as well. In the market-place or inn they are given tips, or drinks. 'It is not necessary to add that their throats, parched perpetually by identical exercises, are equal to the most intemperate intake.'

The songs of the azmaris have played an important part in the traditions of the country, for it is the azmaris who are the carriers of the epics of the past, along with the story-tellers. When they sing of the past, they are preserving it for the future. Many of their songs are handed down, and have been handed down for centuries. Moreover, the themes of the songs often stem from medieval times or even earlier. Improvisation on a popular theme easily leads to the over-simplification or dilution of the theme, so that the historian cannot rely on the azmaris for historical veracity; nevertheless, they provide the germs of history while stimulating the patriotic fervour of their audience. But much of the azmari's verse and music 'feels the effect of the improvisation from which it springs. He has the lot of our executants: little of his endures.'

So, in his role of singer, massenqo-player, historian, political and social commentator, and entertainer, 'the azmari is sought after, and dreaded, for his spirit'. Or so he was—for as already mentioned the twentieth century is ousting him. Many of these troubadours were killed by the occupying army between 1935 and 1940, as each was a strong patriotic rallying-post. There still are some azmaris who can entertain in the Imperial palace, though much of the sting is of necessity taken out of their songs as power is delegated to the self-conscious commons. There still are some azmaris who go to the houses of the great noblemen, though the more sophisticated a Ras's household grows the less welcome is a relic of the past. There still are some azmaris in the towns, but they no longer roam the country-side widely. In fact, today the Ethiopian minstrel sings only at weddings and domestic celebrations, by and large. The musical heritage of the country will lose more than can ever be recorded if the day comes when the last azmari sings, in inn or at court: and the massenqo, chiefly the instruments of the azmari, will take a long step towards the world of instruments of the past.

(ii) In the azmari we find on the highlands of Ethiopia a twentieth-century parallel with medieval Europe; in the *Lalibalas* we have a group of minstrels the like of which probably has never existed elsewhere in the world.

To avoid confusion it is well to call these minstrels by the plural form, *lalibalotch*, as Lalibala is the name of the twelfth-century king who is supposed to have organized these singers into a guild;[1] it is also the name of the village in Northern Ethiopia renowned for its monolithic rock-hewn subterranean churches, which were carved out at Lalibala's instigation.

The lalibalotch were lepers, and many of them still are. In Europe in the Middle Ages a leper was a shunned person, condemned to beggary and a life of separation. 'In our old Gascony, the Cagots or Capis could not mix with the people; they had a quarter marked off by chains, they could use only certain washing-places, and they had a special corner reserved for them in the churches.' But in Ethiopia many of them joined the guild of lalibalotch, and even today the

---

[1] This section is considerably expanded from Mondon-Vidailhet, p. 3181.

lalibalotch sing at dawn as they have done for eight hundred years.

Being thus grouped together, the lepers naturally inter-married. Leprosy is not hereditary, but, although the sons and daughters of the lepers like as not were entirely whole persons, they tended to remain in the community with their relatives, cut off from the world at large.

Yet they are not entirely cut off. In any village on the plateau you may hear the songs of the lalibalotch in the hour before sunrise. If you were abroad you would see shadowy figures grouped at the gateways through the fences that surround every Ethiopian home, and especially round the gateways of the rich. Their faces are almost completely wrapped in the long traditional cotton shamma, or shawl, that is the universal garment of the Ethiopians, leaving only their eyes exposed. As dawn is about to leap up with tropical abruptness these lalibalotch slip away into the shadows: unrecognized, not wanting to be recognized. At the same hour the next night they re-appear; and always before they leave they receive the alms—scraps of food, or money—that are sent out to them by the master of the house.

Nobody knows who the lalibalotch are. You may see a severely-afflicted leper in the street, but you do not know if he was one of the singers at your door that morning, for not all lepers are lalibalotch—nor are all lalibalotch leprous. In the daytime all the lalibalotch except the obvious sufferers take their place as ordinary members of the village, tilling or working at some trade. They do not reveal themselves as the dawn singers, and probably no one wants to identify these singers. But nobody sings their songs except the lalibalotch themselves, and you will not find a lalibalotch song included in any programme of folk music. Their songs go unrecorded, tainted by the disease which taints so many of them; but passed on from generation to generation in this unique brotherhood.

Mondon-Vidailhet thinks that 'it is only the lalibalotch

who, from an artistic point of view, merit our attention', when studying Ethiopian music. This goes rather far in denying the value of other types of Ethiopian music. Doubtlessly the songs of the lalibalotch would reward their student with a wealth of material, if it were possible to find the lalibalotch and talk to them; but they go unknown, and unseen except for their enveloping clothes. One could hide a microphone by the gate and catch some of their songs; to do more than that, to persuade them to reveal their secrets, would require patient work to obtain their confidence. 'It must be realized that . . . the most original element in contemporary Ethiopian music remains accessible only to musicians possessing a certain quality of heroism': a gallicism that need not deter the musician who has the time and the patience, rather than the heroism, to face this fascinating subject.

Men's and women's voices are to be heard in this strangest of dawn serenades, singing in a duet or even a trio of a particular type. The women sing first, then the men, and then both together.

It is hardly more than homophonous music. It is a very simple form of harmony, usually based on the third, dominated by a melody full of vocal turns perfectly executed. Is it the hour of dawn, when the gloom begins to pale before the rising sun? Is it the melody itself, which is not unmelancholy? Is it this simple harmony, simple yet perfectly suited to the singing of feminine voices? I do not know. But I may say that the impression one gains is soft and sad, and I have not known a single European, even those who show themselves the least sympathetic to Abyssinian music, who has not appeared to be moved, to a greater or lesser degree.

(b) The Zafan

Zafan is an Amharic word meaning secular song and dance. The Ethiopian sees no need to separate the two. It is quite foreign to him to stand or sit still while he is singing, except in songs in which the singer accompanies himself on the krar, massenqo or baganna. These latter do not come under the heading of zafan. Although zafan refers both to song and to dance, this section deals with song only, some additional information on the dance being added in section (f) of this chapter, below.

Zafan are nearly always performed by men and women together.[1] The whole company claps hands vigorously throughout; an atamo or other small drum might be used as well. Repeatedly the women break in with shrill ululations, 'ley-ley-ley-ley-ley', in a joyous and ecstatic fashion. This cry is a secular relic of the religious Semitic 'Hallel', or 'Alleluya'. The song is a solo with oft-repeated refrain, and intoned cries of 'Ah!' or 'Ey-hey!' at the end of each line generally add to the enjoyment of the participants.

The verses of the zafan as often as not are traditional ones, as often as not are improvised. Even if they are improvised the extemporization is done in the folk idiom that has endured for centuries; thus in both types we find all the virtues of simple folk-songs. They are short, unpretentious, eminently enjoyable, and above all close to the people and their way of life. They are the true folk-art of the country, a living fount from which new streams are always flowing. Although the Ethiopian church has had a music notation system for at least six hundred years, and possibly for sixteen hundred years, zafan have never been written down: few peasants would have learnt to read with any fluency, let alone tried to master the much more difficult notational skill, the secret of the priests even today.

Folk art is the product of the daily lives of the people, and in the zafan we can see reflected every aspect of this life. Many of them are work songs, on a wide variety of themes but each one associated with some task or other. Some are for picking the coffee, plucking the cotton,

---

[1] This section refers mainly to Mondon-Vidailhet, pp. 3180–2, and Pankhurst, Chapter XXIII.

harvesting the corn, weaving the shamma-cloth, churning the butter—the list could be extended considerably. Others are songs about daily tasks, to be sung while reminiscing at home; and as they are sung the performers go through the actions, fitting the dance to the verse. There are humorous songs about love, and love-stricken songs too; there are songs of joy and sorrow, defeat and victory, storm and sunshine, lullaby and excitement. The Ethiopian's nature is as volatile as the Latin temperament, and his bubbling sense of fun often shows itself in zafan that gently satirize the master of the house, the local nobleman, the busybody, or the incompetent. Time and again we find that improvisation is the keynote: improvisation that is cleverly done, with the ease of constant familiarity, for these songs frequently are newly-wrought words fitted to a well-proved tune.

Spontaneity is the key to improvisation. There must be the spontaneous impulse to sing before the new version of the old song can spring into being. Men going home from work will break into song, led by one of their number, re-creating wittily and concisely some event of the day. Schoolboys who have won a football cup will seize the trophy and set off round the field, singing a wildly impetuous chant that, verse by verse, mentions every member of the team, and their coach, and their school, and the incompetence of their opponents.

As was stated in the Introduction, Ethiopian music is rhythmically very simple. This feature is typical of the simplicity of the zafan. As so much of the verse has to be improvised, and has to be shaped by the tune that already exists for it, there is no chance for rhythmic variations to develop. Neither is there any need. The pleasure the zafan gives to its humble performers is twofold—in the appreciation of the skill of the versifier and in the actual chorus singing and dancing—and no third element is needed. Perhaps too much attention is paid to the words and not enough to the music, from the musician's point of view.

The melodies that are currently popular at one time are overworked with a constant supply of new words until many of them fall into disuse, their place being taken by other melodies. This is what leads Mondon-Vidailhet to complain of a lack of musical vitality, and to suggest that the lalibalotch alone merit the musician's attention. There is some truth in what he says; but the zafan does not exist for the muscian to study—it exists to satisfy the ordinary people, who make it and go on making it to their entire pleasure.

In the examples given here of zafan, the words have been put into straightforward English, while keeping roughly to the form of poetry.[1] The first one is sung by a woman, and the chorus joins in with the last phrase of every line.

> When I asked for him at Entoto he was towards Akaki—
> > so they told me;
> When I asked for him at Akaki he was towards Jarer—
> > so they told me;
> When I asked for him at Jarer he was at Mendar—
> > so they told me;
> When I asked for him at Mendar he was towards Awash—
> > so they told me;
>
> . . .
> > . . .
> > > . . .
>
> When I asked for him at Jibuti he had crossed the sea—
> > or so they said.
> I sent to find him a hundred times, but I have never
> > discovered him.
> I sit by my fire and weep.
> What a fool he is to hope he will ever find anyone to
> > equal me!

Added fun is obtained if the joke in the song can be directed against someone related to a member of the chorus, or to the singer herself, as in the following one. She is

---

[1] They are quoted from Pankhurst, pp. 416ff.

protesting about the utter worthlessness of her husband, and
the song is a good illustration of the clever use of ideas
even in a simple zafan. Perhaps to give the soloist time to
improvise the next line the chorus would repeat each line
after her.

> Trousers of wind and buttons of hail;
> A lump of Shoa earth, at Gondar nothing left;
> A hyena bearing meat, led by a leather thong;
> Some water in a glass left standing by the fire;
> A measure of water thrown on the hearth;
> A horse of mist and a swollen ford;
> Useless for anything, useful to no-one—
> Why am I in love with such a man as he?

Each of those lines offers the same implication about the
unreliability and uselessness of the man, but some are more
obscure than others. It would only be a fool who would
think of carrying a lump of earth from Shoa province to
Gondar, and when he had done the 300 miles there would
be nothing left; only a fool would use a hyena to transport
meat—the beast would eat the leather thong as well as the
meat; 'a horse of mist' shows us the fool chasing a horse
although the only horse there is is a swirling shape in the
mist. 'A swollen ford' is explained as a translatable example
of a pun. 'The French adjective "débordé" can be used to
describe both a river in flood and a dissolute man, which
the words "a swollen ford" imply in this song.'

These two examples were extempore zafan, which were
captured and preserved. Most of them, however, are as
short-lived as is the inspiration that gives birth to them,
and the zafan-singers see no need to remember their songs
when there are always more to be made.

Marcel Griaule found that singing is used as a lure by
the hippo-hunters on Lake Tana.[1] His Waito guide took
him in a frail tankwa, or papyrus-reed boat, to a suitable

---

[1] See *Abyssinian Journey*, pp. 190 ff.

spot near the shore of the lake. Then the hunter began to sing 'in a great clear voice a song of peace in the dead tongue of the Waitos'. Much of it was addressed to the hippos:

> My father hippopotamus,
> My little father,
> Bring your children some food!

He was sitting in the bow of the boat with his legs crossed under him, his chest bent towards the water as for a sermon. The melody was broken by rapid recitatives which left him breathless. His voice carried over the wavelets to the banks of papyrus which bordered the edge of the lake, into the creeks where the animals slept.

As the Waito went on singing first one hippo's nostrils, then another, and a third, appeared in the water, till there was a small herd, all approaching the singer.

> Forgive us for loving you so:
> Your meat is so good,
> My little father!

The hippos drew to within 20 yards, but the hunters did not shoot, much to the Waito's surprise. Then, informed of the nature of the song and the number of the men, the animals vanished one by one.

'What do you say to that?' asked one of the Europeans.

'Curiosity pushed them on,' answered the other.

'And you,' went on the first, speaking to the singer, 'tell me why the beasts came so near.'

'Because my song is the song of our fathers and has always drawn beasts from the water.'

Unfortunately for the Waito's faith in his song, the European drew out a referee's whistle, and began blowing strongly. Soon the boat was again surrounded by hippos; but the Waito could not believe it.

(c) The Fukara

The *Fukara* are a type of secular song especially sung by warriors. Mondon-Vidailhet wrongly transcribes this name as 'fahura'.[1] These fukara are quite distinct from the songs of the azmaris. The latter may be patriotic in spirit and full of praise for the glorious deeds of the past; but the warrior songs are a proud boast. Indeed the word 'fukara' itself means 'vow'.

These songs are most typical of Gojjam, the province from which many of the fiercest soldiers come, and where much of Ethiopia's inherited culture is preserved.

Nowhere is gallantry more highly valued; nowhere is gallantry more braggart or more exuberant. The Abyssinian conqueror feels the need of celebrating his exploits. Hence we have the fukara, which is the most expansive expression of his natural boasting. In several fiery verses he expresses everything that he believes himself capable of, and everything of which he judges the rest to be incapable. All this bears much resemblance to those songs in which Homer's warriors congratulated themselves while they provoked their adversaries.

Most of a fukara song is sung at full voice. The boaster is accompanied by a massenqo or krar, usually the former, and possibly by thunderous drumming. On his arm he carries his round shield; in his belt there is a long thin curved sword; his right hand carries a 10-foot spear; over his shoulders a great cape is flung, and on his head he flaunts a whole lion's mane—in former days won by his own spear. Improvisation being the essence of so much Ethiopian music, he struts up and down, hurling taunts at his opponent and singing his own praises. The opponent, real or imaginary (nowadays the latter), might be a wild beast in the chase, or a whole platoon of enemy soldiers. As the singer reaches a climax, another warrior suddenly takes up the theme, of course trying to exceed the first singer with details of his own past and future exploits. All this arouses the surrounding fellow-soldiers to a pitch when they too want to rush off immediately into the fray; but a third warrior interrupts, scorning the first two and all

[1] See Mondon-Vidailhet, p. 3181, for references in this section.

others as well. So it builds up to a tremendous climax of noise and excitement, when the singing degenerates into shouting. The effect of these warrior songs is very powerful, even in the modern world of the concert hall. One can well imagine that these songs never would be performed in peacetime in the villages, or else the villagers would be so aroused that they would seize the nearest weapons and all rush off to fight a non-existent enemy.

(d) The Mousho

Funerals are noisy events in Ethiopia, it being considered that the grief of the mourners is in direct proportion to the amount of wailing and singing. Even at the funeral of humble people professional wailers may be found. At more important funerals, and especially at the Tezkar memorial services on the 12th, 40th, and 80th days after death, lamentations are composed and sung. This singing is the task of a woman leader supported by a choir, the Amharic name for which is *Mousho*.

These lamentations concentrate only on the virtues of the dead person. 'I have heard of wives thus celebrating, beside the corpse of their husband, the virtues more or less actual that they attribute to the deceased.'[1] The choir repeats the refrain after each couplet, or repeats the couplets themselves, which generally are composed of alexandrines. The singing is accompanied with gentle hand-clapping, or the beating of an atamo or other small drum. As the song comes to an end, the refrain is repeated again and again, and each time one more singer drops out, like an oriental 'Farewell Symphony', until there is only one voice left, intoning the last refrain in a soft diminuendo.

Some of these laments are of considerable poetic interest.

---

[1] See Mondon-Vidailhet, pp. 3181–2 and Pankhurst, pp. 418–19 for the material on which this section is based.

They may be improvised, to a well-known tune; but as a good length of time elapses between the burial and the Tezkar gatherings, there is time for these laments to be composed in a more thoughtful manner, and set to new melody. A fine example was composed by the daughter of a man named Sabagadis, who was killed in a civil war in 1831.[1]

> Alas! Sabagadis, the friend of all,
> Has fallen at Daga Shaha by the hand of Wubshet.
> Alas! Sabagadis, the pillar of the poor,
> Has fallen at Daga Shaha, weltering in his blood.
> The men of this country will ever remain good,
> Because they will eat corn which has sprouted in his blood.
> In November, at the feast of St. Michael, who will remember?
> Mariam, with five hundred Gallas, has killed him.
> Who will remember the loaf of bread and the glass of wine?
> The friend of the Christians has fallen at Daga Shaha.

The phrase 'In November, at the feast of St. Michael, who will remember?' reminds the audience that alms should be given to the poor on that day—but now that 'the pillar of the poor' has been slain who will do it? The penultimate line is the most complex, and is explained by Pankhurst thus:

The loaf of bread and the glass of wine may be assumed to represent both a gift to the poor and the provision of bread and wine for the Communion service. Ethiopian poetry is intensely symbolic; profound significance is attached to the bread and wine; the daughter of Sabagadi thereby invokes his memory as one who was abundant in virtue and human kindness, tender to misfortune, faithful in religious observance.

This is another daughter's lament, composed by the daughter of a man who had been Governor of Simen and died in Tigre. It was sung to the baganna, with the mousho choir as well.

---

[1] First quoted in *Journal of Three Years' Residence in Abyssinia*, by S. Gobat (London, 1833), p. 251.

When sorrow penetrates the heart of man,
It is the moon who comes to shine on him.
Lest you should see the sorrow that is mine,
Oh that the darkness might be more profound!
My grief will never end;
My lamp sheds its last rays, and is extinct,
And oh the land of Simen is so far!

The mousho choir is not associated only with funerals. Often it has a place in hunting scenes, when a lion or elephant has been killed and the hunter returns to the village. Now is the time for a quick-minded extempore paean, the soloist first giving out the refrain which is to be chanted after every line, and then setting out on an interminable round of verses.

According to Mondon-Vidailhet, the mousho 'even turns to parody, and reproduces genuine fables, in which the characters are usually monkeys, or mice, or other animals of that sort. These little scenes give much amusement to the women and children, and are one of the most curious features of popular music.'

The Dorzai tribe, traditionally the cotton-weavers and makers of shammas, the universal shawl of the plateau, have a unique form of funeral chant and dance. As the funeral procession approaches the church, the menfolk are grouped round and in front of the coffin-bearers. All are singing loudly and apparently joyfully: the sound certainly does not seem to be one of sorrow. In the vanguard there is a single dancer, leaping and tumbling and prancing. Amongst the singers perhaps two or three very high tenor voices stand out well above the rest, repeating a three-note descant figure. One singer leads the verses, probably in extempore praises of the dead man, and the whole group joins in the chorus, which comes in fragments at the end of each line as well as in full at the end of the verse. All are singing strongly, contrasting markedly with the solemn and rather subdued chanting of the debteras at the funeral service later, on the steps of the church. The effect is that of a three-part choir, as the solo voice begins his next line while the chorus are still in the middle of their ritornello, and the descant continues all the time. At the end of the song, the men all break into an energetic dance, following the leading dancer right round the church in the middle of the church compound. All go on singing the chorus as they dance. The women take no part in this performance.

I have often heard this Dorzai funeral chanting, and every time I have been very struck by its character, quite unlike any ordinary Ethiopian funeral, the latter for solemnity matching any funeral in Europe. The explanation given me, which at least seems possible although I cannot vouch for it, is that the Dorzai Christians think it stupid to mourn for a man. One should rejoice, for the dead man is now happy on reaching the next world that is every man's goal. To mourn his leaving this miserable world would be mere selfishness.

(e) The Leqso

A remarkable feature of Ethiopian music is the *leqso*. This is 'a sort of complaint associated with a year of sorrow, or with a more or less tragic event'.[1] Mondon-Vidailhet compares the leqso to the 'vocerie' of Sardinia and Corsica, songs of sorrow and vengeance sung by the women: but in Ethiopia they are valued as a highly-developed art. A typical leqso consists of

joining together in a couplet, or better in a sort of elegy, one or more puns, sometimes macabre, addressed to one of the notables of this world. Spoken or sung in a certain way, the couplet seems to celebrate the virtue of the person; lengthen the sound of a letter, modify a soft or hard consonant, and the abuse appears, often caustic, sometime cruel. This conceit is very greatly appreciated in Ethiopia, and it is the women of the aristocracy that excel in it remarkably. All this is

---

[1] See Mondon-Vidailhet, pp. 3181-2, Pankhurst, p. 418, for sources for this section.

repeated and sung by the women and perhaps a choir, in a manner according to the importance attached to it.

Thus the leqso is an intellectual skill, evanescent but satisfying, in which the music is of secondary importance. 'A well-fashioned leqso is worth more than a long poem or song', and some leqso spread quickly throughout the country if their aptness is notable or their victim unpopular. If any instrumental accompaniment is used, it usually is the krar.

I could not find an example of the words of a leqso that related to a definite event. The following quotation serves only meagrely to show what a leqso is like, and of course it loses its impact as soon as it is translated from the Amharic of its originator, Tsegaye Gabre Medhin, who improvised it at a moment's notice.

> Behind the churchyard is heard a trembling:
> I guess it's so-and-so calling to his friends.

The 'trembling' is as of bushes in the wind; but the implication seems to be that the trembling might be 'so-and-so' whispering to his friends, the evil spirits, or trembling with fear because he is so cowardly, or even calling to the dead people in the graveyard whom he is soon going to join. This inadequate example does not convey any of the acidity of a real leqso.

(f) Secular Dance

As has already been indicated in section (b) of this chapter, dancing is especially associated with the zafan, or ordinary folk-song of the highlands people. Dances are never performed as an entity in themselves. They always are a part of a song. The dance may be going on while the song is being sung, or during the chorus; alternatively it may be an interlude between verses, or a long-drawn coda. But no matter where it comes it is an integral part of the zafan;

and just as in the zafan words and tune are often improvised, so is the dance, within certain stereotyped limits.

Intricate footwork or body movements is not typical of Ethiopian dancing. In general, movement of the body from the waist to the knees is frowned upon, especially for women, and most attention is paid to the neck or shoulder dance. The women excel at this. It consists largely of 'a sort of ungainly dislocation of the neck, moving forwards and backwards and involving a certain movement of the breasts'.[1] The shoulders may click back and forth together; then the dancer clicks one shoulder many times rapidly, and suddenly the head moves apparently from one shoulder to the other, although it remains in its usual vertical position. All the while the dancer puts hands on hips, and eager clapping and drumming pound out the four-square rhythm. Occasionally the dancer slowly flexes the knees almost to the ground, but always she stands on the same spot, perhaps faced by a man going through the same energetic movements, and certainly surrounded by a chorus of villagers clapping and singing. There may even be three dancers in the circle, but not more: dancing is not done in large active groups. The 'ley-ley-ley' cries that point the climaxes in the zafan are very much a part of the dancing, being used to encourage the performers to ever more violent contortions of the upper body.

A. J. Hayes watched a group of women dancing on the east shores of Lake Tana.

The dancing of the women seemed to me not unlike that which is customary in Egypt and the Soudan. The chief feature of it was the protruding of the chest and chin alternately. The more forcibly this was done the more excellent was the style of the dancer. During this performance they gasp like whirling dervishes.[2]

In Gojjam province, the men take a much more prominent part in traditional dancing than do the women. One man

---

[1] Mondon-Vidailhet, p. 3180.
[2] *The Source of the Blue Nile* (London, 1905).

begins to leap into the air, wriggling his shoulders and neck as he does so. Then other men join in, each trying to excel the others in athletic achievements. They perform this leaping dance so energetically that it cannot be kept up for more than a few minutes at a time. Meanwhile, the women sing and clap hands, and if they join in the dancing it is more demurely, without the leaps.

In gatherings of Galla people the dancing differs somewhat. A woman dancer puts her arms round the shoulders of two other women for support; she then stamps her feet very hard on the ground, both together, with a deep outgoing breath which is forced through her clenched teeth in sharp 'tss-tss-tss' sounds at each foot-stamp.

4 *Ecclesiastical Music*

(a) Notes on the History of the Church and its Culture

The Christian Church in Ethiopia is a member of the family of monophysite or orthodox Eastern Churches. It should not be confused with the Coptic Church of Egypt.[1] In this book it is referred to simply as the Ethiopian Church. The other Eastern Churches are the Syrian, Melchite, Armenian, Coptic, and Slavonic. The Greek Orthodox and Russian Orthodox Churches are closely related.

The early history of Christianity in Ethiopia is straight-forward. It may be dated from A.D. 327, when King Erzana was converted, and the following year, when Frumentius, a Syrian or Phoenician, was ordained in Alexandria and sent as bishop of 'this centre of African Hellenism'. About A.D. 500 another mission was undertaken by Syrian monks, but it was finally the Hellenic influence, or rather the Coptic influence, which was important in shaping the liturgy.[2] The country has remained Christian ever since, although passing through the vicissitudes outlined in Chapter 1 (*c*), and has until the past decade been under the sovereignty of the Coptic Church, through the appointment of the Ethiopian patriarch from Alexandria. Rey summed up the Christian history of Ethiopia, thus: 'They profess the same religion as

---

[1] 'Copt' is a mutilation of Greek 'Aigyptos' and of Arabic 'qibt', and means Christian Egyptian. See the *New Oxford History of Music*, Vol. II, Chap. 2.
[2] Ibid., pp. 47–50.

that of Europe, acquired when the Europeans were still pagans, and retained in what they believe to be an older and purer form'.[1]

Apart from these facts there is little agreement, little certainty, about the Ethiopian Church's inheritance and cultural relationship with other Eastern Churches. There is only a maze of suggestions, many of them contradictory, some uninformed, and all hindered by an almost total lack of research into one of the most revealing features of the Ethiopian Church, its music.[2]

The entire liturgy of the Ethiopian Church is chanted, except for the Scriptures themselves, which are read. This chanting is certainly exceedingly old, but there is disagreement about its origins, and the origins of the notational system by which it is preserved. It is a firm Ethiopian belief that both the chant and the notation were invented as a result of divine inspiration working through St. Yared, in the reign of Gabre-Maskal (A.D. 550–70).[3] Other sources suggest that Yared only composed the original chants, and that these were handed down orally till the middle of the sixteenth century, when two priests named Azaj Gera and Azaj Rageul introduced the notation.[4]

However, the chanting of the Ethiopian Church is usually thought to owe a great deal to yet earlier origins than Yared, even if Yared did compose new chants or rationalize the existing ones. The chanting has definite links with Old Testament Jewry. Ullendorff lists[5] an impressive series of instances that show an indisputable inheritance in the Ethiopian Church from Judaism, without it necessarily being clear who were the carriers of these influences. These include the shape of the usual Ethiopian church, which

---

[1] *The real Abyssinia*, p. 39.
[2] For an outline of research done from 1650 to the present century, see *New Oxford History of Music*, Vol. II, pp. 47–50. The list is very small indeed.
[3] Cheesman, op. cit., p. 377.
[4] *Grove*, Vol. II, pp. 868–9.   [5] Ullendorff, Chap. V.

resembles the Jewish temple; the importance vested in the Ark of the Covenant (the tabot), as was so for the Ark of the Tabernacle in the Jewish temple; the existence of two distinct orders in the Ethiopian Church, the priests and deacons who officiate at the Mass, and the *debteras*, who are the musicians and teachers;[1] the Ethiopian baganna, probably a form of David's lyre, now secularized but still associated with Lent and serious themes; and the dance of the priests in front of the tabot, as David danced before the Ark. 'The Abyssinian rite certainly kept more closely than any other to the earlier pre-Christian ritual of the country. The ecstatic style of dancing is only one of many signs of this.'[2]

Curt Sachs has drawn attention to another obvious link, concerning the performance of the Ethiopian chants: 'There is a trait reminding us of the Jewish temple: the ends of the line are marked by shaking the sistrum, be it the ancient Jewish sistrum or more probably the ancient Egyptian sistrum, which in its native country has been forgotten.'[3] Geographically the Ethiopians may have got their sistrum from Egypt; culturally they took its usage from Judaism. Further suggested links are the eight-day circumcision custom, common only to the Jews and Ethiopians; the regular weekly fasts on Wednesday and Friday, just as the Jews kept Monday and Thursday; and the emphasis laid upon church teaching, as happened in the synagogue.

These very considerable Judaic elements in the Ethiopian Church today must be syncretic relics from pre-Christian Ethiopia, and were not imported into Ethiopia as a feature of the incoming Christianity, itself to some extent an amalgam. 'It would be inconceivable that a people recently converted to Christianity should *thereafter* have begun to boast of Jewish descent and to insist on Israelite connexions,

---

[1] See also Pankhurst, p. 232.
[2] *New Oxford History of Music*, Vol. II, pp. 47–50.
[3] *The Rise of Music in the Ancient World East and West*, p. 97.

customs, and institutions.'[1] It is by no means incredible to suggest that Ethiopian chant may have Judaic roots.

Strong though these pre-Christian influences may have been, once Christianity began to spread the influences from Eastern Christendom were immense. 'Early Ethiopian Christianity had to borrow extensively from foreign sources in inaugurating a traditional ceremonial, organized monasteries, sacred music, ecclesiastical architecture, and decorative design; but out of all these influences there emerged an integrated system whose pattern was distinctively Ethiopian.'[2]

Doctrinal conflicts in the early Christian churches of the world led to the monophysites rejecting the Council of Chalcedon (A.D. 451) while recognizing those of Nicaea (325), Constantinople (381), and Ephesus (432). The heretics, as they were then considered, took refuge in Egypt, Arabia, and Ethiopia, and thus Ethiopia was firmly orientated towards the churches that grew up in these countries, her geographical and spiritual neighbours.

The Ethiopian Church's contact with Middle-East Christendom may be summarized by pointing to trading contacts (as are witnessed by ancient Greek, Sabaean, and Ethiopic inscriptions); to the first bishop, who was sent from Alexandria, as were his successors; to the sixth-century expedition sent by the Ethiopians to help the Christians of South Arabia; to the sixth-century Syrian monks, the so-called Nine Saints, who brought with them revered manuscripts for translation into Ethiopic; to a steady stream of Ethiopian pilgrims to the Holy Land; and to the Ethiopian monastery which even today is to be found in Jerusalem itself. It was through the Holy Land link in particular that Byzantine art was able to influence the Ethiopian Church. But we must not put too much emphasis on these contacts: communications were so slow, and Ethiopia was so inaccessible across the huge deserts and

---

[1] Ullendorff, p. 100.   [2] Doresse, op. cit., p. 83.

escarpments, that no overseas influence was more than tenuous.[1]

(b) The Ethiopian Notation System

The notation system used in Ethiopian church manuscripts consists of a line of Ge'ez or Ethiopic syllabic characters, combined variously with certain curved signs, dots and dashes, written above each line of the Ethiopic text of the liturgy, the hymns, and the psalms. The letters used as musical symbols are called *milikit*, and the signs *seraye*.

Some authorities who have studied the wide variety of Ethiopian manuscripts now lodged in various museums and libraries in Europe have stated categorically that to avoid confusion the text is written in black and the letters and signs of the notation in red; others that, to avoid confusion, the letters of the notation are in black, and the signs in red; or that, to avoid confusion, the signs are black and the letters red. To prevent further confusion, I must record that it is impossible to generalize about this. The thick volume of hymns that I studied in the library of Holy Trinity Cathedral, Addis Ababa, was written throughout in a manner that does not correspond with these statements. On many pages, alternate lines of the text, or pairs of lines, are in black and red. On the first page, part of which is reproduced in black-and-white at Plate 11, there are even groups of three or four black lines of text interspersed with pairs of red lines. All the notation, both letters and signs, is black throughout, even when the text also is black, except that in just a few instances, when there is a compound music symbol, part is written in red. I was assured that no rule governs the use of red or black, which are selected entirely at the artistic whim of the debtera writing the manuscript; nor has there ever been a rule. It is noteworthy that in the volume I studied each group of lines in the first column was

---

[1] See Pankhurst, pp. 129–30.

exactly matched by a similar group in the second and third columns, obviously for artistic effect.

Further confusion arises from the fact that the signs, as distinct from the letters, that are used in the notation system are sometimes referred to as neumes. A neum in its usual sense has a definite time value in relation to its fellows, and a pitch value in relation to its fellows or to the stave upon which it is placed. Neither the signs nor the letters in the Ethiopian system have any time or pitch value, whether in relation to each other or to their position above the words of the text. I would suggest, therefore, that it is just as misleading to call these signs, or the letters, 'neumes' as it is misleading to use 'mode' for the three styles of melody.[1] We should rather speak of the milikit, the characters which comprise the milikit being letters and signs.

The letters are the most important part of the notation. Each letter means not one note but a whole group of notes, extending at times to a phrase that in European notation would take up perhaps two or three long bars. Each letter, or pair of letters, is an abbreviated form of a whole phrase or line of text to which a particular melodic phrase was sung. The letter hence comes to refer not to the text but to the melodic phrase to which that text was set. When the letter is placed above a word or phrase of another line of text, it signifies to the cantor that he must sing this fresh text to the melodic line that belonged to the text indicated by the letter. Thus each original phrase of music has its own milikit, consisting of one or more Ethiopic letters taken from the original text; and each milikit could be used with any text at will, if new hymns or settings of the liturgy were being composed, or for ecclesiastical poems.[2]

Detailed illustration of this process is set out in Mondon-Vidailhet's work,[3] using Ethiopic script with French transcription. This is probably the most easily studied example

---

[1] See section (c) of this chapter.   [2] See section (f) of this chapter.
[3] p. 3193.

using the vernacular. The milikit method may well be illustrated, avoiding the complexities of the Ethiopic syllabary, by supposing the adaptation of the system to English.

Ex. 15

In the Church of England chanting of the psalms, the tune set out in Ex. 15 is often associated with verse 1 of Psalm 42:

Like as the hart de-/sireth the / waterbrooks: // so longeth my soul/ af-ter / Thee, O / God.

We must assume that this is the text for which it was composed, and that the one is always associated with the other. If we wanted to use this tune for another verse, it could be identified by selecting a letter (or two, or more) from the text of the verse, and putting it (or them) above the text of the new verse. The melodic line up to the double bar might be represented by L (Like) or LK (LiKe), or by the first and last letters of the whole group of words, LS (Like . . . waterbrookS); the choice would not matter so long as it was quite distinct from any letter or combination of letters ever used for any other phrase. The first two bars after the double bar might be SL (So Longeth), and the last two bars OG (O God). Taking verse 3 of the same psalm, in the Ethiopian notation system the melody of verse 1 would be fitted to it thus:

L   SL

My tears have been my meat day and night: while they daily say unto

                OG

me, Where is now thy God?

Usually the milikit letter is placed at the beginning of the textual phrase, but not necessarily always on a strong-accented syllable, or even on the first syllable of the phrase.

As each milikit letter can only have one musical meaning, there is no need for a stave, whose basic use is to show the melodic rise and fall for a series of single notes in western notation.

The milikit signs serve to instruct the singer in how to interpret the melody. They are the equivalent of phrase-marks, slurs, staccato and glissando marks, and so forth. In western music, one singer might slur an interval which another sings staccato: they have each sung the same melody but interpreted it differently. The milikit signs are the Ethiopian interpretation marks. They are as follows. (The signs might be used in combination. For example, at (ix) the combination of (ii) and (vi) is written.)

(i)   •   (*Yizet*): stop, or pause, or breathe.

(ii)   ‿   (*Deret*): drop the voice to a deep chest register.

(iii)   ⌢   (*Difat*): two notes of the melody dropped to a lower voice register.

(iv)   ⌡   (*Chiret*): downwards glissando on 'ah'.

(v)   ⌊   (*Kinat*) upwards glissando on 'ah'.

(vi)   —   (*Heedet*): quickly, accelerando.

(vii)   ⊦   (*Kurt*): cut the note short, staccato.

(viii)   ... or ⁚   (*Rukrik*): repeat the note several times in rapid succession on the same syllable (ፇ)

(ix)   ‿—   combination of (ii + vi): drop the voice and move more quickly.

At the beginning of each hymn or portion of the liturgy, a symbol is placed to indicate which of the three 'modes' is to be used.[1] In addition, there may be some instructions

---

[1] See section (c) of this chapter.

about speed, such as *meregd* (slow and even), *nius-meregd* (quicker), *abiye-tsefat* (still quicker), *tsefat* (presto).[1]

The system is simple, once it is explained. The difficulty lies in the fact that there are so many different milikit, all of which need to be learnt by heart if a debtera is to be able to read any music manuscript at sight. The Ethiopic syllabary contains 202 characters.[2] If the letters were only used singly, there would be 202 different melodic phrases at most; but they are often used in pairs, occasionally in threes. Obviously the number of possible permutations and combinations of 202 symbols singly, in pairs, and in threes is a huge total, so that in theory there could be an incredible number of different melodic phrases to be learnt. Villoteau gave a list of some 47 which he had collected from Ethiopian priests he met in Egypt; H. Zotenberg found 168, which he merely listed, in the manuscripts in Paris;[3] Mondon-Vidailhet printed 15 signs and 43 letters,[4] some of his signs seeming not to exist and some of his letters being wrongly explained, as far as I could ascertain. Halim El-Dabh[5] thinks there may be as many as 300, while as a very tentative estimate I would suggest that a figure of even 600 might not be too high. Given time and patience enough, one could work right through all the volumes of manuscripts that constitute the entire corpus of Ethiopian sacred music, both liturgical and hymnal, and build up a vocabulary of milikit. These could then be recorded one by one and transcribed into western notation. It would be an immense task. It would also be of academic rather than practical interest. 'I even believe that

---

[1] See Pankhurst, p. 241.

[2] The Modern Amharic syllabary, which is directly descended from the Ethiopic, contains an additional 74 characters. See *A History of Ethiopia*, pp. 555–6.

[3] *Catalogue des MSS Ethiopienne de la Bibliothèque Nationale, Paris* (Paris, 1877), p. 76.

[4] pp. 3194–5.

[5] He is working on a detailed study of the notation system at the Haile Selassie University, Addis Ababa.

ECCLESIASTICAL MUSIC

a serious study of Ethiopian plain-chant notation would demand prolonged work perhaps out of proportion to its real value.'[1]

Ethiopian notation takes its place alongside the other notation systems of the world's diverse cultures, past and present. To link it definitely with others is difficult, but indications can be made of possible connection.

'It is probable that the earliest attempts at notation were made by the Hindus and Chinese, from whom the principle was transferred to the Greeks.'[2] The exact nature of the Greek notation system is not settled, and various authorities say that the Greeks used 1,680, 1,620, 990, or 138 signs in their alphabetic system. The Romans developed a quite different system, using 15 letters of the Roman alphabet for the scale of sounds within two octaves. This was the end of the alphabetic system in Europe.

In Europe the neumic system evolved over a long period, stretching from the earliest use of dots, dashes, hooks, curves, and strokes in the sixth century down to the final five-line stave and measured notation system a thousand years later. The neumes were 'in the first instance merely rough expression marks placed over the words, to guide the singers of the plainsong melodies, the melodies themselves being learnt by ear, and hence they have no indication as to the pitch or time-relation of the notes.'[3] Later the musical intervals were suggested by the distance of these signs from the words of the text—the first step towards using guide lines (i.e., the stave).

Notational systems are to be found in manuscripts belonging to nearly all the Eastern Churches. These systems are generally known as ekphonetic notation, a name introduced when the cantillation, or quasi-chanting, of the lessons in the Byzantine liturgy was being studied in the 1880s, 'Today when we use the terms ekphonetic chant and

---

[1] Mondon-Vidailhet, p. 3180.   [2] *Encycl. Brit.*, Vol. XVI, p. 21.
[3] Ibid., p. 256.

ekphonetic notation we understand by them the solemn reading of the lessons and the signs used to regulate its performance in all the eastern churches.'[1]

Ekphonetic notation systems are very primitive. They consist of a limited number of conventional signs designed for the solemn reading of a liturgical text. Originally they were merely accents indicating the raising or lowering of pitch, or signs calling for special inflections used to bring out grammatical peculiarities such as questions, exclamations, affirmations, and so on. Their development into more elaborate formulae is now obscure. They occur in Byzantine, Armenian, Syrian, and Coptic manuscripts of the later Middle Ages, from the seventh to sixteenth centuries. In Jewish chant a similar system is used to this day. This Jewish chant, 'usually referred to as cantillation, consists of successions of stereotyped melodic formulae, each of which is represented stenographically by a sign written above or below the scriptural texts'. The oldest extant source for these accents (ta'amam) is a ninth-century manuscript.[2]

Full details of the various ekphonetic notation systems may be found in the *New Oxford History of Music*;[3] but a few brief comments may be of value.

The Syrian system was simple, consisting mostly of dots placed above, between or below the words of the text. It supposedly dates from the late fifth century. The Byzantine system, originating towards the end of the fourth century, was much more complex. It had two forms: simple symbols for the formal reading of lessons, and a more advanced system for the singing of hymns. The Armenian system is the least understood. As early as the fifth century it used letters; by the twelfth century it had developed into an elaborate neumic system, similar to the Byzantine.

The chant of the Coptic Church had no notation system,

---

[1] The full reference is given in the *New Oxford History of Music*, Vol. II, Chap. I.

[2] Brit. Mus. 44451. See *Harvard Dictionary of Music*, pp. 235 and 380.

[3] Vol. II, Chap. I : see especially pp. 35–41, 51.

but was handed down orally.¹ However, Halim El-Dabh drew my attention to a manuscript, now in the Metropolitan Museum, New York, which until recently was in the Cairo Museum. This is supposed to be a Coptic manuscript of the first century A.D. It makes use of a notation system based on circles of various sizes and colours, indicating seven different tones. This manuscript is not mentioned in the standard works of reference, but it may well be a most important link in the ekphonetic chain. According to *Grove*, in manuscripts of the texts of Coptic hymns each item is 'preceded by a few words which are to be regarded as indicating the melody to be used, as was the custom in the Greek school of hymn-writing'.² It is also stated there that there was apparently no notation known today, but there was 'some slight use of simple ekphonetic notation'.

Before any wholly tenable conclusions can be reached about the development of the ekphonetic systems, and of the Ethiopian ecclesiastical notation, a very large amount of work has to be done. It is severely hampered by lack of manuscripts in many fields. Moreover, lack of original writings on the interpretation of the existing manuscripts means that we have no contemporary authorities on whom to base studies today. It is not safe to rely upon twentieth-century interpretations of early manuscripts, even when made by priests or scholars of the church whence they originated; as so many of the chants were handed down orally for century after century their performance was bound to undergo some metamorphosis, just as a folk-tale is modified through the generations. Even supposing that the ekphonetic systems had not themselves been modified, but had remained constant, the fact that they were not a complete record of the chant means that today's interpretation of yesterday's system could not be historically accurate, because of oral modification of the chant traditions.

It used to be supposed that neumic notation originated

---

¹ Ibid., Chap. 11.   ² Vol. II, pp. 860 ff.

in Rome or Constantinople. The discovery of the Syrian system of ekphonetic notation has destroyed that legend. Study of the Ethiopian and Jewish systems of notation suggests that the ancient Babylonian script may well have a musical interpretation. If it really was a notation system, the date of the earliest musical accents would be pushed back by more than a thousand years, well into Old Testament times.[1]

Ethiopian notation rises above the level of ordinary ekphonetic notation in that it is the most developed Eastern system, and extends to all the music of the church, not just to the cantillation of the lessons. Wellesz suggests that the Ethiopian system, with its combination of letters and signs, is derived from two sources. 'Perhaps the religious cleavage, which is reflected in the Abyssinian Mass, and which had its origin in the clash of evangelizing forces, the Syrians and the Copts, finds its expression in this double system of notation also'.[2]

(c) The Three Ethiopian 'Modes'

Reference may be found in several earlier writers to the three 'modes' of Ethiopian liturgical chant. These modes have been a cause of much discussion, without any clear understanding of their true nature. The following account is based upon detailed questioning of Kagn Geta Mesfin Hailemariam, a debtera at the Theological College, Addis Ababa, who is a specialist in ecclesiastical chanting and teaches it to the students. I believe it to be correct, no matter how much it may cut across what more learned authorities than myself have said.

The three modes are called *'Ezel*, *Ge'ez*, and *Araray*. Each name is associated with a particular *mood* or manner of chant, the three being quite distinct from one another.

---

[1] See *New Oxford History of Music*, Vol. II, Chap. 2, and *The Rise of Music in the Ancient World East and West*, p. 97.
[2] *New Oxford History of Music*, Vol. II, pp. 868–9.

The *Ge'ez* mood is the simplest. It is relatively plain and unadorned chanting. Mondon-Vidailhet thinks it may well be the oldest (and therefore it may bear the closest resemblance to Jewish Old Testament chanting). He bases this partly on the name itself; for this is the name of the dead language, also called Ethiopic, that holds the same place in the Ethiopian Church as does Latin in the Roman. The Ge'ez tongue and script is the oldest in Ethiopia, probably coming from the Agazizan tribe, one of the many Semitic tribes who migrated in pre-Christian times.[1] More important is Mondon-Vidailhet's suggestion that 'greater simplicity is a sure sign of greater antiquity'.[2]

The *'Ezel* mood is very serious and heavy-sounding, slow and dignified. It is particularly associated with the chanting for fasts and vigils, and at funerals. It tends to keep in the lower register of the voice.

The *Araray* mood is lighter, gayer, altogether more free. It goes up to the highest notes of the voice, and is a more complex melodic line, full of appogiaturas, grace-notes, and other dexterities.

For the most part this explanation coincides with what Mondon-Vidailhet says.[3] It might well help to remove future misunderstandings if the word 'mode' was no longer used of Ethiopian liturgical chant, for 'there is nothing in Ethiopian music that resembles major or minor modes, or the different modalities of our plain-chant'.[4] If the word 'mood' is so close to 'mode' as to cause confusion, we might talk of the various 'manners', or even 'humours', for instance.

Previous ideas that the so-called modes indicated various note-rows were probably based on Villoteau's work at the end of the eighteenth century. *Grove* quotes the conclusions reached by Fétis, who from Villoteau's work deduced the

---

[1] See Budge, *A History of Ethiopia*, Vol. I, pp. 120–1, 130.
[2] p. 3192. [3] Ibid. [4] Ibid.

three scales set out in Ex. 16 (a). *Grove* adds that the araray scale should run as in Ex. 16 (b), 'if based on a correct interpretation of the melodies'.[1]

Ex.16 a

Ex.16 b

The *New Oxford History of Music* merely states that 'the basis of Ethiopian music is the three modes. . . . The meaning of the names is obscure. Villoteau mentions that the *ge'ez* mode was used on weekdays, *araray* on the great feasts, *'ezel* on the days of fasting and mourning'.

Ullendorff points out that 'a similar division exists also in the case of the Hebrew *niggunim*, which vary in very much the same manner' as described earlier in this section.[2] If a connection could be clearly established between Ethiopian chant and the niggunim, it would indicate a much earlier origin for the three Ethiopian moods than their supposed origin, St. Yared, in the sixth century.

(d) The Legend of St. Yared

There is evidence that suggests quite strongly a pre-Christian origin for much of the Ethiopian system of chanting. This rests chiefly upon the three moods, ge'ez, 'ezel, and araray. These are unlikely to have sprung suddenly into being in the sixth century with the arrival of Yared, the supposed originator. It is far more plausible to suggest that

---

[1] See Vol. II, pp. 868–9; also Fétis, *Histoire de la musique*, Vol. V.
[2] Ullendorff, p. 173.

they grew up gradually, through century after century. It is true that the strongest cultural link is to be found between the Ethiopian Church and the other Eastern Churches, especially the Syrian and the Coptic; but no similar system of moods of chant is found in the chanting of those churches. Thus the Ethiopian moods more likely come from the old Hebraic cantillation. The notation system is a possible further Hebraic link, though only tenuous, through pre-Christian ekphonetic notation. Moreover, the melodies of the church are thought by some authorities to have a definite Jewish element. At this point it is as well to consider the legends that surround Yared, and the part he is said to have played in the foundation of Ethiopian ecclesiastical music.

Yared is dear to the heart of every priest and debtera in the Ethiopian church. The full story of how he created the whole of the chant of the church is set out in the *Senkessar*, or Ethiopian Synaxarium (The Lives of the Saints). This document dates from the end of the fourteenth century. This abbreviated account is taken from the full-length translation given by Mondon-Vidailhet.[1] The legend exists with many variants outside the Synaxarium, but all have the same purport.

Yared is believed to have been born in Simen.[2] He was not an apt pupil-debtera, and was beaten so much that he fled. In the desert he saw a caterpillar repeatedly falling from a tree it was trying to climb; but finally it got to the top. This so inspired the youth that he went back to his master, begged for forgiveness, and set to work again.

His brainpower was greatly increased, and he learnt in one day the Old and New Testaments. After this, he was named deacon.

At this time, there were no rules for the famous *ziema*, or liturgical chant. The offices were recited in a low voice. But when the Saviour

---

[1] pp. 3189–91.
[2] It is significant that the supposed originator of Ethiopian music was born in the province which 'for centuries has been the stronghold of Hebraic tradition'.

wanted to establish sacred chant, he thought of Yared and sent three
birds to him from the Garden of Eden, which spoke to him with the
language of men, and carried him away to the heavenly Jerusalem,
and there he learnt their chant from twenty-four heavenly priests.

On his return to earth, he set to work composing a large
number of chants for the hymns and liturgy of the church.
These he sang in a voice as beautiful as the voices of the
birds that had come to him.

And when the king and queen heard the sound of his voice they were
moved with emotion and they spent the day in listening to him, as did
the archbishop, the priests and the nobility of the kingdom.

And he appointed the chants for each period of the year, whether
it be the summer, winter, spring, or autumn, for the Sundays and the
festivals of the angels, prophets, martyrs and the just. He did this in
three modes: in ge'ez, 'ezel, and araray; and he put in these three
modes nothing far removed from the language of men and the songs
of the birds and animals.

The story describes how Yared was so moved with the
Holy Spirit when he sang that he did not even feel a spear
which accidentally pierced his foot. Yared became a monk,
and died an unknown death.

Cheesman, the great authority on Lake Tana and its
many island churches and monasteries, visited Tana Kirkos
Island, on the eastern shores, where he found some interesting relics. 'We next examined the clothes of Arad
Kahn, alias Yared the Deacon, who lived in the reign of
Gabre Maskal. These vestments, in brightly coloured cloth,
are still worn in church ceremonies by priests in attendance
on the Ark.'[1] It does not seem likely, to say the least, that the
vestments he saw really had survived 1,400 years and still
were in use; but the fact that the priests believed it so shows
the veneration held for the Saint.

The chronicles praise the superlative quality of his chants.
He made chants 'the like of which was not to be found in

---

[1] *Lake Tana and the Blue Nile*, p. 177.

the East or in the West, neither among the Romans nor the Greeks nor the Syrians nor the Egyptians.'[1] 'Nobody can invent a new mode which could be added to the three modes of the priest Yared.'[2] Yared is credited not only with the creation of the whole method of chanting: some chronicles even say he was the inventor of the notation system as well, this being revealed to him in a moment of divine inspiration.

This over-enthusiastic support accorded to Yared even extends to at least one twentieth-century writer. 'All agree that it was in the sixth century A.D., in the reign of the Emperor Gabre Maskal (550–564), that Yared, a learned Ethiopian ecclesiastic, invented a method of writing Ethiopian music, which previously had been transmitted orally and had been preserved from generation to generation by memory alone.'[3] There is no general agreement, not even among the Ethiopian manuscript sources, let alone those who have studied Ethiopian music, but only contradiction. However, this quotation is more important in that it introduces a new idea, unfortunately without supporting references, namely that Yared only codified the traditional chants which 'previously had been transmitted orally'. If this is right, it is certain indication that the basis of the chants, if not the chants themselves, is pre-Yared, that is, pre-sixth century. Do we take this to indicate that the chanting came in with the Christian influence of the Coptic and Syrian churches, from 327 to the sixth century? Did the chants come earlier to Ethiopia, with immigrants from Semitic Arabia? The lack of references is distressing.

Mondon-Vidailhet contributes helpful though inconclusive comments on the possible derivations of Ethiopian chant.

Ethiopian plain-chant approximates more to the ecclesiastical music of the Syrians or the Armenians; it seems to me also to have—although

[1] Quoted in *Grove*, Vol. II, pp. 868–9.
[2] Quoted in *New Oxford History of Music*, Vol. II, pp. 47–50.
[3] Pankhurst, p. 238.

in a small degree—some sacred songs that we hear in Jewish syna-
gogues. The vocal flourishes are more abundant: they characterise in
some degree the Abyssinian plain-chant. Although the Ethiopians
claim that their music has a national origin, it seems to me that it can
be related to the music of these ancient churches, particularly the
Armenian, and also the Egyptian. . . . The Ethiopian priests maintain
that it was only the notation that was introduced at this time (i.e., of
Yared). The 'mamher', or doctors, have assured me that the chants of
the psalms, such as are preserved in Ethiopia, have a Judaic origin,
and reproduce the Hebraic chants of the time of David and Solomon.
I give this information in passing: I will not debate it.[1]

In the collection of manuscripts in Paris, there is one
which Mondon-Vidailhet summarizes. 'In the time of
Emperor Galawdewos two priests appeared, Azaj Ghera
and Azaj Ragouel, learned in musical affairs. They began
to introduce notation into ecclesiastical chant and instructed
in it all the priests of a certain monastery.' If this were
right, it would place the introduction of notation between
1540 and 1559, the dates of Galawdewos' reign.

It is, however, wholly unlikely that Ethiopia had not before this
possessed an adequately regulated liturgical chant. It must be a
question of some reform such as that which St. Gregory introduced
in our plain-chant, perhaps the introduction of letters and of groups of
letters beside the neumes,[2] more primitive than ours. . . . It is to be
noticed that the title Azaj, prefacing the name of the two priests, is a
civil title, corresponding to our 'manager' or 'organizer', and I do
not know that there exist in Ethiopia any priests bearing this title.[3]

So Yared, we find, is variously given credit (a) for invent-
ing the notation system by which it became possible to
write down the chants that in the sixth century were already
traditional; (b) for creating the three modes or moods; and
(c) for composing the entire body of liturgical music. To
assess his place accurately in the development of Ethiopian

---

[1] p. 3189.
[2] What he calls 'neumes' here are what I have called 'signs' above.
[3] pp. 3191–2.

church chant is impossible for want of real evidence; but it seems reasonable to suggest he was a gifted debtera who, working with a traditional type of chant that already was firmly established, composed a good number of new hymns and anthems. Possibly he was the first consciously to fit music to the mood of the occasion; or possibly he was the first to collect and arrange the inherited types of chant into the three modes, that had always existed in the spontaneous growth of the chant but had never before been recognized. Possibly he developed a primitive form of notation, which was the foundation upon which the sixteenth-century innovators built. It all is conjecture, informed by a few historical facts, as Mondon-Vidailhet says.

The Abyssinians have dedicated to the birth of their plain-chant a certain number of legends, which are not designed to clear away the mists in which it is wrapped.[1]

(e) The Church Scene in Ethiopia

The highly individual Ethiopian ecclesiastical chant is set against a church scene that is just as remarkable. 'Ethiopia is a country of churches. Their number is immense.'[2] In spite of Muslim destruction of large numbers of churches about 1540, Ethiopia still has so many as to attract the attention of many travellers.

There is no country in the world where there are so many churches as in Abyssinia. Though the country is very mountainous, and consequently the view much obstructed, it is seldom you see fewer than five or six churches; while the view from a commanding point will probably include five times that number.[3]

In proportion, the number of fast-days in the year seems just as high. Ullendorff, probably the most authoritative writer on Ethiopia today, says that 'the total number of

---

[1] p. 3189.　　[2] Ullendorff, p. 109.　　[3] Bruce, op. cit., p. 125.

fasting days amounts to about 250 a year, of which about
180 are obligatory for all'.[1]

The churches are either square or circular, the latter shape
being the more common in Ethiopia, and unique in
Christendom. In each case they are divided into three
sections, one inside the other. The outer section or passage
extends right round the building. Laymen and women come
into this part, and the debteras sing here. The middle section
is where the drums and sistra are kept, and where lay people
come to take Communion. The innermost section is where
the Ark or tabot is kept. Only priests may enter here. The
altar is of wood, covered with an altar stone, with a represen-
tation of the Ark of the Covenant, and draperies richly
embroidered as in the Temple of Solomon. The walls are
painted, but never sculptured.[2]

These three sections bear Ethiopic names very like
Hebrew words. The second chamber, 'keddest', is equivalent
to the kodesh of the Tabernacle or the hekhal of the Temple
of Solomon; the holy of holies in Ethiopic is 'keddusa
keddusan', which is 'kodesh hakkodashim' in Hebrew. The
shape of the church is the Hebrew one, in contrast to the
basilica accepted by early Christians elsewhere.[3]

The walls of the churches often are decorated with vivid
paintings, in the same style that illuminates many manuscripts. With the bright colouring and rather naïve stereotyped figure-drawing they are reminiscent of Byzantine
painting, but opinions differ as to the extent to which they
are derivative, as also about the style of architecture.

There seems no doubt that not only Coptic and Syrian craftsmen but
also Europeans filtered into Ethiopia at different times and made their
distinctive contributions to the development of local art. There were
Florentines who arrived in 1402, and the Venetian Brancaleone fifty

---

[1] p. 106; Dr. L. Krapf said in his *Travels* (1860) that the total fasting
amounted to nine out of the twelve months; Rey said in *The Real Abyssinia*
there were 150 days.
[2] Pankhurst, p. 167.   [3] Ullendorff, p. 109.

years later, who introduced a number of sacred figures characteristic of Graeco-Italian iconography. But they were all more or less completely assimilated and very soon forgotten.[1]

The churches must have looked as colourful in their heyday as did the great European cathedrals. Alvares mentions going to the Giorgis Church at Genata, and seeing its glorious panelled walls, and paintings covering the entire interior, executed by Brancaleone. The doors were not just gilded, but were overlaid with thick gold leaf.[2] But nowhere are statues to be found in Ethiopian churches. 'Nothing embossed or in relief ever appears in any of their churches, for this would be reckoned idolatry; but they have used pictures in their churches from a very early period.'[3]

The two schools of thought about the effect of foreign influences on the development of Ethiopian church art are summed up in these contrasting extracts. Sylvia Pankhurst's opinion is that

in studying Ethiopian art and architecture one is constantly impressed by the fact that Ethiopian art is extremely individualized and differs in many respects from every other type, both in pre-Christian and Christian times. It is generally accepted that the art of Ethiopia was largely evolved by her own builders and craftsmen. A style peculiar to Ethiopia can be traced from century to century from early Christian times onwards through the Middle Ages.[4]

But Sir E. A. Wallis Budge, of the British Museum, studied the large numbers of Ethiopian manuscripts deposited there, and concluded that the pictures, typical of Ethiopian church art,

were not of native origin (though their painters copied faithfully enough native objects, inanimate and animate), and that the artists must have had copies of some kind to work from. . . . All the available

---

[1] Doresse, p. 207. This Brancaleone was also known in Ethiopia as Macureo or Macureos. Fr. Alvares called him Nicolas Brancolian, 'a very honest person, and a great gentleman, although a painter'. (*Narrative of the Portuguese Embassy to Abyssinia*, trans. Lord Stanley, 1881). See also *Legends of Our Lady Mary the Perpetual Virgin and Her Mother Hanna*, trans. Sir E. A. Wallis Budge, 1933, pp. xii–xiii.
[2] Quoted in Doresse, p. 207.　[3] Bruce op., cit., p. 127.　[4] pp. 129–30.

evidence suggests that colour pictures were first introduced into Ethiopian manuscripts in the fifteenth century, and that the European element in them was derived from the pictures that were painted on the walls on the churches by . . . Brancaleone . . . who lived in Ethiopia for forty years.[1]

The manuscripts are highly valued by the Ethiopian Church. The oldest extant date probably from the fourteenth century, although many are copies of translations into Ethiopic from Arabic or Coptic as early as the seventh or sixth centuries. The existence today of the Book of Enoch in the Apocrypha is due only to the discovery by Bruce of one manuscript of it in Ethiopia, the only one known. Collections of manuscripts, many of them with the full notation system, are available in many European centres.[2] Every church in Ethiopia has its own library of manuscripts some of them of great value, and jealously kept away. The monasteries and island churches on Lake Tana did not lose so many treasures as did other regions in the Muslim invasions.

A great deal of devotional literature and music is inspired by the Virgin Mary, who is more venerated in the Ethiopian Church than in the Roman. Whole volumes of the praises of Mary are chanted or read every year, being divided into separate sections for every day of the week. There are over thirty festivals annually dedicated to her. Translations of some of this great corpus of literature have been made, and show an ecstatic emotion and strength of imagery often paralleled in the Old Testament. The extract given here[3] is a good example of the typically biblical language that is

---

[1] *Legends of Our Lady*, pp. xii–xiii (see footnote 3 below).
[2] British Museum approx. 500; Bodleian, Oxford, 100; Biblio. Nat., Paris, 688; also in Berlin, Vienna, Frankfurt, Jerusalem, Windsor Castle, Cambridge, and the British and Foreign Bible Society. Each MS. is a whole volume, which may well be several books.
[3] From *Legends of Our Lady Mary the Perpetual Virgin and Her Mother Hanna*, trans. Sir E. A. Wallis Budge, pp. 297 ff. See Brit. Mus. MS. Orient. No. 559, fol. 125 ff.

standard throughout the Ethiopian liturgy and much of the hymnary.

She is the ship of gold that cannot be moved among the raging billows and waves, and her raft is bound with the ropes of the Trinity, which cannot be separated. And she is also the pillar of pearls which cannot be moved by the might of the winds; there is neither falling nor shaking for him that leaneth upon it.

Let the mouth of everyone who readeth this book be seasoned with the salt of divinity, and flavoured with wild honey in the comb and the juice of sugar.

I have found thee a refuge from the corruption which is upon the earth and from the punishment which is for ever. I have found thee a refuge from the lions of the north, which roar mightily and snatch away with violence, and hunt the young and show no mercy upon the old, and gape with their mouths to swallow up their prey. I have found thee a refuge from the evening wolves, which do not pass the night in sleep till the dawn, and they seize and carry off and leave no sheep untouched, and they spare neither the young goat nor the lamb. I have found thee a refuge from the face of the bow and from the mouth of spears and swords, and from every instrument of war. I have found thee a refuge from the hands of all mine enemies, and from the hands of all those who hate my soul. Who can strike terror into him that putteth his trust in thy name? And who can make afraid him that taketh shelter in thy name? The roaring of the lion one may liken to the yelp of the dog, and to him the strength of the panther is as the feebleness of the cat. The onset of horses cannot reach him, and the flight of the arrow cannot come near him. The mouth of the spear cannot wound him, and he can look upon the casting of the stone as a thing of naught. The flooding of the rivers cannot cast him down. The tongue of man hath no power to vilify him; and the lips of the man of oppression cannot do him harm, for he cannot conquer thy Son when he argueth the case with Him. This is my knowledge.

(f) The Training of the Ethiopian Church Musician

It has been suggested that as many as one-third of the population of Ethiopia are priests, deacons, *debteras*, or monks. At a lower level an estimate of two million has been given.[1] All these members of the Church have at least some knowledge of church music. Many more children attend the early stages of church schools, although of course not all proceed to the rank of deacon or debtera, remaining lay members. Thus the church and its music are a very vital element in the culture and society of Ethiopia today—as they have been for a thousand years at least—influencing a very large section of the community.

The lower hierarchy of the priesthood is in four divisions.[2] The first division attends a church elementary school, learning the Ethiopic script and language, studying the Acts of the Apostles, and chanting the psalms. The second and third are the diaconate and priesthood respectively. The debteras, or church musicians, are on a level with the priesthood but do not enter Holy Orders.

Even today it is possible to be ordained into the diaconate with little education, although the standard is rapidly rising. Bruce's description of an ordination in the 1770s must be taken with a certain amount of scepticism, as must many of his rather exaggerated observations, but it is still of interest.

A number of men and children present themselves at a distance, and there stand in an attitude of humility, not daring to approach the Abuna (Bishop). He then asks who they are; and they tell him they want to be deacons. On this, with a small iron cross in his hand, after making two or three signs, he blows with his mouth twice or thrice upon them, saying, 'Let them be deacons.' I once saw the whole army of Begemder made deacons, just after a battle in which they had slain about 10,000 men. The Abuna stood at the Church of St. Raphael in Aylo Meidan, about quarter of a mile from them. A thousand women, who were mingled with the soldiers, got the benefit of the same blast and brandishing of the cross, and were made as good deacons as the rest. A somewhat similar form is used in the ordination of monks, who, however, are required to be able to read a chapter of St. Mark.[3]

---

[1] G. Harmsworth, *Abyssinian Adventure* (London, 1935), p. 228.
[2] Cheesman op. cit., p. 103; Pankhurst, Chapter XV.
[3] Bruce op. cit., p. 127.

The preservation of the musical culture of the Ethiopian Church rests almost entirely with the debteras, who undergo a rigid system of education that raises them intellectually a good way above many of the priests. The latter chant the Mass (Khedase), and this is not studied by the debteras; they chant it with less skill than the debteras devote to the rest of the church singing.

After the debteras have completed the ordinary elementary school course, their training involves an impressive amount of memory training. The various stages are the School of Music or Song (Ziema); of Dancing (Aquaquam); and of Poetry (Kene). In addition, some go on to study in the School of Theology and History (Matsahaf).[1]

In the Ziema, the debtera has to study the whole of the Ethiopian antiphonal, or collection of hymns. There are at least five great collections of hymns, for various seasons of the church's year.[2] The *Deggwa* alone is a thick volume, divided into sections called 'Yohannes' (for the New Year), 'Meraf' and 'Tsomadeggwa' (for Lent), 'Astemeru' (for between New Year and Lent) and 'Fasika' (Easter). The *Mawasat* are anthems for the whole year; the *Egziabehr Nags* anthems are for the Saints' Days; the *Gubae Malke* are general hymns; the *Zimare* are for the dead; and there are others too. Study of these works in effect means learning them by heart. A fully-qualified debtera is completely conversant with the notation system and every one of its several hundred symbols; but the studying is so lengthy that he rarely needs to refer to the music manuscripts once he has completed his course—he has committed the entire melody of the ecclesiastical chant to heart. He may use a copy of the text, but the milikit are largely superfluous.

Part of the process of memory training is the copying of the manuscripts of the entire antiphonal. Each debtera is expected to make his own copy. This involves him in making

---

[1] See mainly Mondon-Vidailhet, Section 9; Pankhurst, Chapter XV.
[2] See Budge, *A History of Ethiopia*, p. 570.

his own parchment, mixing his own ink and colours, cutting his own quill, copying out the text for every service in the year (except those parts of the mass which never change and are sung by the priests), adding the milikit in hand-writing so small that many European eyes find it difficult to distinguish, decorating the headings, and even illustrating the volume with colour plates if he is able. Then he has to bind the volume in boards covered with leather or cloth, and make a cloth case in which it can be carried about and preserved. This may be as much as seven years' work. It is no wonder that, by the end of it, he has committed nearly the whole of it to memory, for he has also been engaged in constant practice of the singing.

He now knows all about 'raw or unpolished music (tiré-ziema)'.[1] But he has to learn how to accompany the music rhythmically, and how to perform the sacred dances. This is taught in the Aquaquam School. He learns the particular rhythmic patterns according to which the ts'anats'el (sistrum) must be shaken, the mukwamya (a prayer-stick having a long wooden handle and a tang-cross of silver or brass) waved in the air or knocked on the floor, and the kabaro (double-ended drum) beaten. On these rhythms are based the gentle yet compulsive move-ments of the dances that are a prominent part of the big festivals.

There are three rhythm patterns involving use of the sistrum, drum and prayer stick. These are set out in Exx. 1, 2 and 3 (page 20). Any of these patterns may be used in any of the three manners or modes of chanting, and abrupt changes from one rhythm to another are to be found in the middle of an anthem. A fourth pattern involves only the use of the prayer stick, which is held vertically and moved in front of the body and face, away to the side, and down on to the floor, in a slow but fixed cycle of movements that reminds one of a subdued drum-major. The fifth way of

---

[1] Pankhurst, p. 242.

performing the ziema is without benefit of sistrum or kabaro, for use during Lent.

These patterns were all demonstrated for me by Kagn Geta Mesfin Hailemariam. His explanation does not fully agree with the following extract from Mondon-Vidailhet, but it may be taken as authoritative.

The clerks accompany the zemmame singing with light tappings of their canes or crutches, called mukwamya; the maraghed ziema is sung to the accompaniment of the kabaro, or ecclesiastical drum, or of sistra; the tsifat ziema is sung like the preceding one, with the addition of hand-clapping; the dekoussie ziema is, if I am not mistaken, the chant intermingled with another chant, about which I have to present some observations.

The liturgical mass is not exclusively homophonous, and I will record here one of the points which has struck me most. In many ceremonies I have noticed that, before one of the groups has ended its chant, another choir begins its own, in such a way that the ensemble makes harmonized music, a kind of very complicated counterpoint, to which my ear eventually became accustomed, and which it would be very interesting to study.[1]

I was not able to find out anything authoritative about this polyphony, but it seems it might well be the accident of two groups overlapping each other, in antiphony, rather than a deliberate mingling of two choirs in order to produce a short period of polyphony.

The third school of study for the debtera is Kene, or poetry.

Traditionally, all Ethiopian poetry was intended to be sung. In Ethiopia as in ancient Greece poetry was regarded as a branch of music. Just as in ancient Greece there were schools of oral metrical education where the science of sounds and syllables was recognized and taught, so in the Ethiopian Church Schools the science of music and of poetry for singing became long ago an intense and profound study.[2]

In this school the student has to master the art of poetic composition. This of course is a means of acquiring the

---

[1] p. 3192.   [2] Pankhurst, p. 238.

considerable mental discipline to which all poets must submit themselves. In Ethiopian poetry the same qualities are
esteemed as are generally thought valuable in European
poetry, qualities such as economy of expression, aptness of
figurative language, symbolism and allusion, and the
crystallization of experience and wisdom. The debtera has
to learn to write 'language made memorable'. He is taught
as many as ten different types of poetry.[1] Each new kene is
fitted to a melody made out of the existing chants. The
poems are composed to fit into the liturgy at whatever point
they comment upon, for example after the lesson or psalm,
or the homily for a Saint.

A profound knowledge of Ge'ez is the essential preliminary for success
in Ethiopian Church poetry, which must conform to elaborate rules
of prosody. It must never fail in suitability for singing. Moreover, it
must be rich in content, revealing a deep knowledge of the Bible, of
Ethiopian history and of the stories and legends which have gathered
during the centuries around the great personalities and events of
religious and national tradition. Sensibility of the beauty and grandeur
of nature wherein Ethiopia's magnificent mountain scenery is lavishly
endowed, vivid imagination and descriptive power, and the gift of
fine and sonorous language are also demanded. Added to these must
be knowledge of music and aptitude for composition, as all the poems
must be sung.[2]

There are two schools of ecclesiastical poetry. The one at
Gondar 'relies on beauty of melody and rhythm, of phrase
and allusion and upon clarity of expression'. The other, at
Wadela, 'specializes in subtlety of meaning, allusion and
construction, combined with adherence to strict grammatical rules'. 'Silence and profound meditation should
follow a Wadela composition; "Melkam" (praise) should
be heard from the auditors only after a considerable pause,
in contrast to the immediate burst of praise which should
be evoked by a fine Gondar composition.'

---

[1] Set out fully in Pankhurst, p. 244; Mondon-Vidailhet quotes 12 different
types.   [2] Pankhurst, p. 245.

An example of each different type of kene is given in
Pankhurst.[1] Quoted here is one of the briefest, with its
accompanying explanation. It is a good example of kene in
that the poem itself is very brief, and very much to the point
for anyone familiar with the poetry of the Ethiopian Church.
To someone else, however, the two lines need as much as
ten times their volume in explanation, or even more. The
poem commemorates the feast of one of the greatest Ethiopian saints, Abuna Gabre Menfes Keddus, a hermit and an
extremely rigorous ascetic.

Tradition declares that he wept till the moisture of his eyes was dried
and their lustre and fullness was gone. Satan, in the form of a raven,
then pecked them out to tempt him to abandon his faith. This story of
the Ethiopian saint whose eyes ran dry is equated in the poem with the
story of Noah and the flood.

> 'The raven did not return to the Saint, Noah,
> 'Till the water of the eye, the Flood, was diminished
>   from its fullness.'

The Saint is here equated with Noah, not likened to him. Though
this brief form of poetic metaphor or simile tends to be incomprehen-
sible to the European mind, it is well understood and appreciated by
the adepts of the Kene school. The poem as translated here, without
the charm of the original rhythm and the accompanying music,
appears bald. To an Ethiopian the meaning would be approximately
thus:

> 'The raven did not return to Noah till the waters of the flood had
> abated; not till the fullness of the Saint's eyes had been diminished
> by continual weeping were they finally destroyed by Satan, who in
> the form of a raven came to test the faith of the Saint in the Divine
> mercy.'

The devout audience of priests, debteras and laity, being deeply imbued
with Scriptural ideas, require only brief indications to produce the train
of thought the poem aims to arouse.

Without extensive knowledge of Ethiopic a judgement

---

[1] pp. 243–61.

of the kene poems can only be made at second-hand, so Mondon-Vidailhet's opinions[1] contrast satisfactorily with Sylvia Pankhurst's eulogistic remarks.

I must say, in passing, that Abyssinian poetry loses its rhythmic character in proportion as it is further removed from the folk sources, and nears the composition of scholars. The latter has always appeared to me in all respects inferior to the former, whether in rhythmic character or in inspiration; the rhymes are even of a saddening baldness. The singers, or rather the intonants, make up for this imperfection by reciting more quickly those verses in which the length runs far beyond the regular hemistitches.

By the time a debtera has completed all his studies he may have spent at them a total of twenty years after leaving the church elementary school at the age of ten. However, not all debteras pass through the Schools of Song, Dance, Poetry, and Theology. They tend to specialize; some pay little attention to the expertise of the ecclesiastical chant but become theology teachers, while others may become church artists, illustrating manuscripts or doing bright murals in the churches. Thus not every debtera is a skilled church musician; but every church musician is a debtera.

As mentioned earlier in this chapter, the Ziema of the church is divided into various portions. The manner of singing each portion is controlled by a monastery, which is the supreme authority over its particular section, and the preserver of tradition. Mondon-Vidailhet had in his own collection of manuscripts an old chronicle which explained how this divided authority came about.

In the time of King Gabre Maskal, Yared established the Ziema, which endured till Gragne. (This Gragne, also known as the Imam Ahmad, conquered almost the whole of Ethiopia.) The latter destroyed the churches and burnt them, as well as the books they contained.

After the overthrow of the Muslims, all those books which had survived the catastrophe were gathered together, but not a single copy could be found that dealt with the ziema. The King made a

---

[1] p. 3191.

proclamation that he would confer special honours on whoever could present him with an example.

As a result of the search, a etsomadggwa, a meraf and a deggwa were found in the monastery of Betalehem (the Bethlehem of Ethiopia, in the province of Begemder). This is why Betalehem has maintained the privilege of making authoritative pronouncements concerning the deggwa. The zimare (psalmody) and the mawasat (responses), containing the ecclesiastical chants for every festival and the various solemn celebrations, was found at Zour-Amba, as a result of which the monastery remains the authority on matters concerning these two sections. Finally the khedase (the liturgy of the office of the Mass) was found at Selalkon, which remains the principal authority on this matter.[1]

Authority is still vested in these monasteries to this day, which is an added complexity in the lengthy training a debtera has to undergo.

(g) The Dance of the Debteras

The debteras use their drums, sistra and prayer-sticks at every service of the church; but the most impressive spectacle is when they use them at the great Timket festival, one of the major church festivals of the year, when they also dance. Timket is Epiphany, and is treated as the major celebration of that season, Christmas being a much lesser festival.

On the eve of Timket, processions set out from all the churches in a neighbourhood, bound for a common baptismal pool. This may be, as it is in Addis Ababa, a specially-constructed pool, or it may be a pool in a river. In each procession the lead is taken by a kabaro-player. Just behind him comes a priest carrying on his head the tabot, or ark, from the church. So that the eyes of lay people shall not light on the ark, it is completely hidden in long cloths of brilliant red, decorated all over in thread of solid silver or

---

[1] Ibid.

gold. This cloth is embroidered with the most fanciful designs and colours, such that one would think the cloth must have come from the Far East, never crediting that it could be made by simple Ethiopian craftsmen. All around the ark there are the other priests, the deacons, the debteras and the parishioners. Many of the clergy carry ceremonial umbrellas of strongly-contrasting colours, with rich tassels and embroidered like the cloth that covers the tabot. Some carry tall gold or silver ceremonial crosses. The drums beat all the time, and the sistra accompany the chanting as the procession joyfully moves to the place appointed for the Timket festival.

All the arks of the participating churches are gathered in the field of worship and placed in a special tent. Here they are surrounded by priests and cantors, who sing and pray throughout the following night, till the real Timket ceremony begins at daybreak.

The clergy all gather beside the pool and a long service is sung. The water is blessed, and then priests carrying bowlfuls of it move among the huge congregation, liberally sprinkling everyone who is near. The dance follows. The debteras form in two long lines facing each other. Each is dressed in sparkling white ankle-length robes with a turban on his head. The cloth of his robes is embroidered with modest borders. In his left hand he holds his sistrum, in his right his prayer stick. Near by are two or three drummers. The dance starts slowly, with all the debteras singing softly. It consists of a rhythmic swaying from side to side, shifting the balance to one foot as the other is lifted just a little off the ground, and then back to the other side. The prayer sticks are moved back and forth, up and down, raised high, then over to the side, and so on, in a complicated pattern that it is difficult to follow. The 'de-domm' of the tenor-bass double-ended kabaro becomes more excited, the sistra are made to chink more loudly, the pitch of the melody seems to rise higher and higher, the singing becomes louder and louder, the lines of cantors near each other—the whole atmosphere becomes more and more aroused: one seems to be nearing some tremendous climax. But suddenly sound and movement stop.

The first time I was at a Timket ceremony I thought this was just a 'general pause' before the dancers plunged into a wild new dance; but it was the end of the whole ceremony, as abrupt and uncompromising as the end of the first movement of Sibelius' 5th Symphony. Perhaps one is misled by the music, which maybe does not at the end reach what European ears would consider a full cadence; perhaps it is the stance of the dancers in this last moment, with prayer-sticks raised to the sky, and the whole body straining upwards, balanced forwards, that gives the wrong impression. But numerous travellers who have seen this dance comment on the dramatic abruptness of its conclusion. 'Certain travellers have foolishly tried to ridicule these sacred dances; but they could not be more respectable, and do not lack individuality. They are descendants of biblical legends, showing us David dancing in front of the Ark. The tabernacle which contains the tabot, or portable altar, claims to perpetuate the tradition of this Ark.'[1]

The Ethiopian Church also is criticized for the whole essence of the Timket ceremony, by people who say that it is a re-baptism and thus a heresy against the one true baptism. Bruce dismisses this forthrightly: 'A man is no more baptized by keeping the anniversary of Our Saviour's baptism, Epiphany, than he is crucified by keeping His crucifixion.'[2]

As already indicated in the Mondon-Vidailhet extract above, the dancing of the priests has age-old roots.

It obviously comes from Egypt, and was taken up by the Coptic Church, whose rite was closely connected with that of the Ethiopian Church. We may assume that this kind of dancing to the rhythm of rattle and drums goes back to the early days of the church in Abyssinia, for the rattle is derived from the saïschschit of the Egyptians, which

---

[1] Mondon-Vidailhet, p. 3184. [2] op. cit., p. 129.

the Greeks took over and called seistron. The drum has the same egg-shaped form as that of the Egyptian drum, and, like it, was beaten with the ball of the thumb.[1]

There are other festivals at which this dancing occurs. At the end of the season of heavy rains, when agricultural work can be recommenced, there is the festival of Maskal, the True Cross. This commemorates the finding of the true cross, but possibly there are, in the manner of its observance, relics from an earlier pagan end-of-winter rite.[2] These include lavish use of the Maskal daisies, brilliant yellow flowers that carpet the highlands just at this season, and are borne in great bunches at the festival; and a ceremonial procession round a tall stack of wood and flowers, that later is set on fire for the secular part of the festival.

In certain parts, the Feast of Our Lady of Zion is kept as a great festival, especially in Aksum, and the debteras dance as they approach the cathedral church.

Pageantry soars to its noblest heights. Here the choir of debteras, clad in their sacred decorated scarves, intone an expressive chant as they slowly advance towards the cathedral, alternately prostrating themselves and rising again, gesturing in the manner depicted in the ceremonial manuscripts of centuries ago. To the beat of the drums, which are solemn and slow, the clergy advance in two long lines, facing each other in their embroidered capes and snow-white turbans, lifting the sistrum, a legacy of the ancient Egyptians, meeting, cross-ing, and retreating in a very slow dance which dates from time immemorial.[3]

The manner in which the debteras sing certainly strikes strangely upon European ears. Budge's opinion is that 'the voice of the cantor is naturally rough and harsh, and his singing has been described as ill-pleasing'.[4] The debteras nearly always sing at full voice, with no knowledge of voice-

---

[1] Egon Wellesz, in *New Oxford History of Music*, Vol. II, pp. 47–50.
[2] As indeed has European Christmas with its tree, and green leaf decorations, in the home.
[3] Doresse, p. 221.   [4] *A History of Ethiopia*, p. 163.

production such as is considered desirable in Europe, and it is this constant straining that causes the effect criticized by many writers. There seems to be an idea that God's attention is more easily attracted by loud singing. 'Even today the Christian priests of Ethiopia sing in a loud voice until they reach the highest point of ecstasy and are completely exhausted.'[1]

To dislike the chanting, or the dancing, because of its unfamiliarity is not reasonable, for such judgement is clouded by a lack of historical perspective. One must remember that in Ethiopian church ceremonies the unfamiliar was bred in antiquity.

The veneration accorded to the tabot in Abyssinia up to the present day, its carriage in solemn procession accompanied by singing, dancing, beating of staffs or prayer-sticks, rattling of sistra and sounding of other musical instruments remind one most forcefully of the scene in 2 Sam. vi. 5, 15, 16 when David and the people dance round the ark. The entire spectacle, its substance and its atmosphere, has caused all who have witnessed it to feel transported into the times of the Old Testament.[2]

In 1527 a Portuguese Jesuit, Fr. Jerome Lobo, was in Ethiopia. What he saw and recorded then might have been written by anyone going there now, nearly four and a half centuries later.

It is not poffible to fing in one Church or Monaftery without being heard in another, or perhaps by feveral. They fing the Pfalms of David. . . . The inftruments of Mufick made ufe of in their rites of Worfhip are little Drums, which they hang about their Necks, and beat with both their Hands; thefe are carried even by their Chief Men, and by the graveft of their Ecclefiafticks. They have fticks likewife with which they ftrike the Ground, accompanying the blow with a motion of their whole Bodies. They begin their Confort by ftamping their Feet on the Ground, and playing gently on their Inftruments, but when they have heated themfelves by degrees, they leave off

---

[1] Gustav Reese, *Music in the Middle Ages* (New York, 1940), pp. 66 and 94.
[2] Ullendorff, p. 110.

Drumming and fall to leaping, dancing, and clapping their Hands,
at the fame time ftraining their Voices to their utmoft pitch, till at
length they have no Regard either to the Tune, or the Paufes,
and feem rather a riotous, than a religious, Affembly. For this
manner of Worfhip they cite the Pfalm of David, 'O clap your
Hands, all ye Nations.'[1]

(h) Problems in Studying the Music of the Eastern Churches

As I have already indicated, very little study has been made
of Ethiopian church music. This is largely true also of the
music of the other Eastern Churches. It is easy to find out
what each church's music is like today, by just going and
listening; but this only tells how the priests of today interpret the chants handed down to them by the imperfect
means, of one sort or another, used in every Eastern
Church.[2] To discover what the church music used to be
like is almost impossible. It is probable that in musical
aspects, as well as 'in all other aspects of Eastern Christianity, present conditions are but a shadow of their former
splendour, and that only through the medieval manuscripts is
it possible to gauge the wealth and magnificence of the past'.[3]

But there is a very great scarcity of manuscripts of the
finest period. The Eastern Churches possess no editions of
their melodies to set beside those of the Gregorian chant
made by the monks of Solesmes, or of Byzantine church
melodies gradually being published in *Monumenta Musicae
Byzantinae*. These editions have been made possible because
scholars have been able to refer back to Middle Ages
manuscripts, but 'to do so for the Eastern Churches is

[1] *A Voyage to Abyssinia*, by Fr. Jerome Lobo, [translated] by Mr. Legrand
from the French (London, 1735), pp. 61–62.
[2] There is no call for undue satisfaction about the efficiency of European
notations; scholars wrangle about how Bach would have done it, for instance!
[3] Egon Wellesz, in *Grove*, Vol. II, pp. 860 ff.

probably impossible, save for Armenian melody, of which many manuscripts are preserved. All that has been available hitherto . . . has been transcriptions of the melody in the form in which they are sung today.[1]

There is available quite a number of Ethiopian manuscripts of the Middle Ages. There would have been countless hundreds more were it not for the huge destruction done by Gragne's invading Muslims in the sixteenth century. There are a few isolated examples of Syrian manuscripts. Coptic music, as already mentioned, never was written down, unless in the most rudimentary of all forms.

Concerning the style of each separate church's music, it is well to accept the descriptions given by Wellesz.[2] Armenian music 'excels in melodic exuberance and wealth of ornamentation'. Syrian music uses a 'richly varied scale system, strongly influenced by the music of Persia and Arabia'. In Ethiopian music, 'the standard today is considerably lower, but the religious poetry, and such information as has come down to us regarding its music, makes it clear that it stood on a much higher level'. Coptic music is noteworthy for its 'extraordinary richness and expressive power'. The melodies of the Greek Church 'are definitely hybrid in character'. Wellesz thinks that the notion will be destroyed of 'the sterility of Byzantine music, in the same way that modern investigation put an end to the legend of the sterility of Byzantine art. The music of the Byzantine Church indeed is no less great than that of the Western Church; it may even be said to surpass it in its power of passionate expression and its dramatic force'.[3] Finally,

it is most probable that certain of the melodies used in the Mass, either throughout the Eastern Church as a whole or in certain of its branches, have a common origin, and are descended from the earliest Christian times; they may even perhaps be traced back to the melodies sung in the Temple at Jerusalem. This supposition is strengthened by results of comparative research on various Eastern liturgies.

[1] Ibid. [2] Ibid. [3] *New Oxford History of Music*, Vol. II, Chap. 2

5 Concluding Remarks

The culture of the Ethiopians is rich and varied, and for the greater part highly individual. Many examples can be given where the culture is derivative—in the liturgy, in Church customs, in the language and script, in social customs, in painting and architecture, to name just a few—but in almost every case what was derived has in the course of five, ten, fifteen, or more centuries been marked with an unmistakable Ethiopian stamp. This genius for absorbing and making personal a variety of foreign elements is more marked in Ethiopia than it is perhaps in many European countries, where borrowing is on a large scale, and repeatedly the outside influences flood into the native stream and quite overwhelm it. To reach any conclusion about the relationship between Ethiopian culture and the neighbouring cultures is complicated by this disguising of the elements brought in from elsewhere.

These general remarks apply also to the musical culture of the country. Section by section in this book, instances have been given of probable or possible links with other cultures. Without recapitulating the whole list, we have the more obvious examples of the Ethiopian lyre (the krar and baganna); the one-string fiddle (the massenqo); the sistrum (ts'anats'el), prayer stick and sacred dance, and the division of the clergy into two orders, the theological priests and the musicians, teachers, etc. (the debteras). The fact that all these are related in one way or another to Egyptian, Coptic, Jewish, or Greek elements is in no doubt; though it may be difficult to define precisely the manner in which the outside influences came, or whence, in every case.

It seems likely that the ecclesiastical chant and its notation system both have their roots in other cultures, but these roots are more obscure than are those mentioned in the preceding paragraph. This is because so little is known today about the meaning of the old ekphonetic notation systems of the Eastern Churches; so little has yet been published of the Ethiopian notation system; and so few original sources exist to show how the Eastern Churches developed their musical systems. In fact, it may well prove impossible ever to discover the true links between the various musicologies of these churches. At present, few authorities would dispute that Ethiopian ecclesiastical chant has among its roots some that stretch down to the Judaic chants of the Old Testament Temple; one cannot go much further than that general statement.

The amount of work still to be done in the field of Ethiopian music is immense. In writing this book I have had the subsidiary aim of indicating some of the topics and problems. The *beginnings* of a list might include:

(1) making a comprehensive list of the notation symbols of the church chant, transcribing them into European notation;

(2) a search for phrasal similarities between Ethiopian chants and other Eastern church chants (almost a life's work in itself);

(3) the lalibalotch, or leprous singers, and their traditional melodies and verses;

(4) the development of plucked instruments in Ethiopia, Egypt, and Greece;

(5) differences among the instruments in various parts of Ethiopia;

(6) investigation of the four different tuning systems of the krar, to discover the true nature of the various Ethiopian tonal systems.

This is only scratching the surface of Ethiopian musicology;

but it is already a list that demands very extensive work by a variety of specialists.

The Institute of Ethiopian Studies' guide to research work in progress in 1963 included only three people in musicology. These were working on ethnomusicology (the musical instruments); the instruments used for the religious ceremonies, and the musical notes; and church music.[1]

To master any aspect of Ethiopian music, the scholar needs first to study Amharic, with its huge syllabary, and also Ethiopic if he is dealing with church music. The confidence of the priests, monks, and debteras must be gained before manuscripts of real value are brought out. This is not so difficult to achieve nowadays, as there is an increasing number of enlightened scholars in the Church who fully understand the urgent need for the study and recording of this culture. Preparation must be made for travelling hundreds of miles over some of the world's most contorted mountainous scenery, if any truly representative collection of folk recordings is to be made. The ear must be attuned to Ethiopian secular music, so that a sifting can be made, separating the proper folklore music from the westernization that is to be found even in every hamlet, where the radio insinuates the capital's cosmopolitanism.

It is essential to bear in mind the fact of Ethiopia's sheer geographical isolation. The huge deserts, the Rift Valley escarpments, the Nile valley jungles and swamps, and the serrated plateau itself, constitute a formidable barrier holding back foreign armies as well as emissaries of foreign cultures. These features have encouraged the Ethiopians to individualize whatever they have received, as at no time until the 1930's has there been a constant inflow sufficient to dominate their own culture. One must also remember the historical fact of Ethiopia's cultural isolation, surrounded

---

[1] Respectively, Jean Jenkins, of the Horniman Museum, London; Bernard-Louis Velat, of Paris; and Halim El-Dabh, of Haile Selassie University.

for many centuries entirely by paganism and Islam; and of
the overrunning of the country by the Muslims in the
sixteenth century. This was traumatic in its destruction,
though not necessarily resulting in great metamorphosis of
the peoples' culture.

Christians were forbidden to attempt to convert Muslims, to marry
Muslim women, to speak disparagingly of the Prophet or the Koran,
to display crosses, to ring church bells, or in other ways to obtrude their
faith upon Muslims, to erect houses higher than those of Muslims,
to ride thoroughbred horses, or to drink wine in public or allow swine
to be seen. Yet Christianity persisted.[1]

Ethiopian music is perhaps the only large area of African
music that has not yet received the single-minded attention
of great scholars. The music of the Arabic-speaking peoples
has been studied extensively;[2] West Africa has had skilled
musicologists;[3] in South Africa and in Central Africa a
great deal of work has been done;[4] East Africa is receiving
attention; and Hugh Tracey has collected for the International Library of African Music many thousands of
recordings, from all parts of the continent except Ethiopia.
This means that the urgency for study of every aspect of
traditional music is greater in Ethiopia than in other African
countries, for in Ethiopia it is faced with the same degenera-
tive influences as it is throughout the continent.

At present, the traditional music of the plateau is still
quite firmly entrenched in the lives of the people. The
church does not change its chants (though they become
somewhat debased through the simplifying that always
results from orally-preserved tradition: the notation system
is not an accurate record of the melody, but relies upon the
memory of the teacher as to the exact shape of each melodic

---

[1] *A History of Christianity* by K. S. Latourette (London), pp. 320–1.
[2] Notably by Farmer and Newlandsmith.
[3] Especially A. M. Jones.
[4] By Percival Kirby and Rose Brandel, and others.

phrase indicated by the symbols). The azmaris and lalibalotch still sing, or compose extemporaneous songs and
satires. The instruments are unaltered. Song in the traditional folklore style is still a natural expression of almost
every emotion in the peasant. The dances, both of the priests
and of the people, are still performed as they have been for
centuries. And all these elements are well to the fore in any
picture of daily life in a highlands community.

But Ethiopia is becoming westernized at a rate that
alarms many of its older citizens while it does not satisfy
the impatience of its western-educated younger generations.
One hesitates to use the word 'civilized' of this process,
implying as it does a lack of 'civilization' in a country where
we can find preserved the longest-lived Christian civilization
of the whole world. The cultural arts are in many respects
still medieval, whilst in the space of the past thirty years
the country has materially stepped forward many times
faster than ever Europe did. Airlines bring Europeanization
to every part, so that a peasant may find an aeroplane a more
familiar sight than a bicycle. The capital sends out its
Amhara administrators into every corner of the country,
bringing their radios, their education, their sophisticated
twentieth-century outlook and standards. Foreign experts
from every continent spread out through every province,
working in every field of social, industrial, educational, and
governmental service. In the face of all these modernizing
forces, every aspect of the pattern of life is bound to change
very rapidly. What Sharp and Vaughan Williams did for
English folk-song must be done for Ethiopian folk-song
very soon; what the Solesmes monks did for Gregorian
chant must soon be done for Ethiopian chant, if (as may well
happen under the pressure of European materialism) the
Ethiopian church begins to lose its authority and stature.

African folk music is a strong link with African customs. Where the
ancient African culture lives on in accordance with its hereditary
customs, African music also lives on. . . . But the collision between
the African and western ways of life breaks it. . . . African music is

CONCLUDING REMARKS

not a recognized factor in the life of the new African community, the form of which is very largely determined by western examples.[1]

If purely European music were imported into Ethiopia, and kept quite distinct from Ethiopian music, little harm would be done. But the real damage done to traditional music comes from the westernizing of the use of traditional instruments, used now for playing composed 'pop' songs in Amharic as banal as its American or English counterpart; and from attempts to popularize old tunes by playing them with the strictly western resources of a piano-accordion, saxophone, etc. These modern songs are often set to instrumental harmonies entirely foreign to Ethiopian music, and used in a stilted and unimaginative way.

This harmonization results from a mistaken notion that harmonization is in itself a step forward.

The transition from homophony to polyphony in Western music is usually looked on as an advance from a primitive to a more highly developed form of musical expression. This is tantamount to placing the music of the East on the same level as that of truly primitive races, purely on the grounds that its roots are extra-European, and that it does not admit of harmonization. To say that European music represents an advance on that of the East is only partially true. . . . To Oriental ears our melody is weaker and less expressive than theirs.[2]

As the gradual transition from homophony to polyphony took place in European music, 'the creative interests hitherto concentrated on a single voice are dissipated among several'. It is true that a melody accompanied in counterpoint is like 'a jewel enhanced by its setting'; but as a result the melody has to submit to certain limitations. It has no more complete rhythmic freedom, or freedom of decoration. The ornaments that abound particularly in Ethiopian ecclesiastical chant 'represent a principle of construction based not on symmetry but on a melodic line which renews itself in a perpetual flow of exuberant arabesques'.[3] Moves

---

[1] H. Weman, op. cit., Preface.   [2] *Grove*, Vol. II, p. 860.   [3] Ibid.

[129]

towards the harmonization of Ethiopian melodies are a destructive force, and need to be resisted.

Finally, an investigator working on Ethiopian music should not expect to be rewarded with finding music of structural, harmonic, or rhythmic subtlety; but there is much else of great value and interest to be revealed—infinite melodic variation, strongly emotive tunes and verses that spring directly from the volatile and eager spirits of the highlands, and links with the past that may well prove to throw vital illumination on the cultures of other Middle Eastern peoples.

Additional Musical Examples

Many of the recordings were made during performances by the National Folklore Orchestra of the Haile Selassie I Theatre, Addis Ababa, hereafter identified as 'Orchestra'. Examples of Ethiopian music in the body of the book will be found on pages 26, 32, 34, 36, and 38.

Ex. 17. Amhara folk-song about a mother who is mocked for worrying about her son: from a tape belonging to the British Council, Addis Ababa, probably recorded by the Patriotic Association, Addis Ababa.

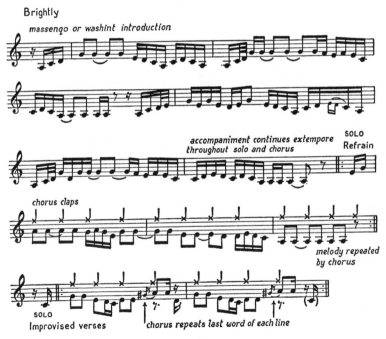

Brightly
massenqo or washint introduction

accompaniment continues extempore
throughout solo and chorus

SOLO
Refrain

chorus claps

melody repeated
by chorus

SOLO
Improvised verses   chorus repeats last word of each line

these two bars repeated ad. lib. with new words; then refrain;
then more verses etc. Chorus repeatedly adds "le-le-le-le."

Ex. 18. Galla song of joy, about love: Orchestra. This song is from Arussi province. The men dance very vigorously as the song progresses, especially in the 2/4 ending.

Ex. 19. 'Almaz': Orchestra. Amhara folk-song, from Shoa province, about a pretty girl who does not take any notice of her admirers.

The solo voice sings the 4-bar melody, repeats it, and adds the 2-bar tailpiece. The chorus follows this exactly. Verses 2, 3, etc. all follow the same pattern.

Ex. 20. Source as for Ex. 6 (p. 36). Probably a Gurage song. This is far removed from any pentatonic idea. Note the emphasis on the augmented 4th F-B. The tenor soloist on the recording sings the top Cs without any strain.

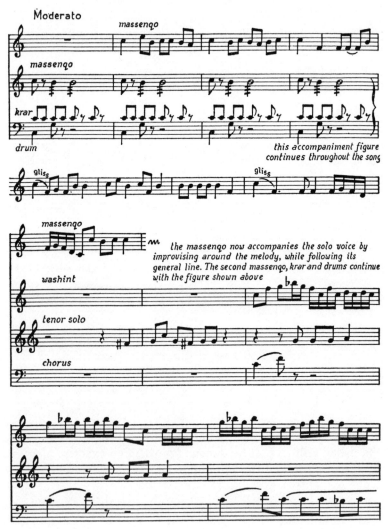

Ex. 20 (contd.)

The chorus and the basic accompaniment remain the same as the song continues; but the washint and massenqo extemporize with increasing enthusiasm as the solo singer develops his theme.

Ex. 21. An ecclesiastical chant: Pankhurst's *Cultural History*. A 'Seatat' melody, or prayer for the night. The drop from E to A in the second line represents a glissando down to a deep and rather indeterminate chest note, and would be indicated by the 'chiret' sign (see p. 93).

Ex. 22. 'Anchi Lidj': Radio Addis Ababa. A modern song composed in the pentatonic folk idiom. It dates from the Italian occupation of 1935–41. The beautiful girl of the song symbolizes Ethiopia.

Ex. 23. An ecclesiastical chant: Villoteau, quoted by *Grove*. Said to be 'an ecstatic piece of Good Friday music'.

Ex. 24. A love song: transcribed by Emile Bloch from a phonograph roll made in Addis Ababa by Prince Henri d'Orléans in 1897, and quoted by Mondon-Vidailhet.

Ex. 25. A love song: Orchestra. A genuine folk-song, bearing the marks of a cunningly composed melody. Throughout, the G sharp is slightly flat to western ears.

Ex.26

Ex. 26. A harvest song: Orchestra. From the Menjar tribe of Shoa Amharas. The soloist is the leader of a threshing party, who all the time go through the various motions of threshing. The words are improvised around the quality of the harvest, the good fortune of the farmers, the characters of the harvesters, and any other topic which comes to mind. The song becomes faster and faster, as the soloist improvises around the various themes, and ends when all are exhausted. (See facing page.)

Ex. 27. Galla war song: Orchestra. Each warrior boasts of his past accomplishments in the hunt or on the battlefield, and his superiority over any possible enemy or colleague. As each succeeding warrior reaches the shouting stage, the others join in, at first with exclamations of astonishment, and then with reiterations of their own prowess. There is no set melodic line, but each singer displays the greatest coloratura bravado of which he is capable. On my recording the top Cs and Ds are easily reached by the soloists.

The soloist's improvisations grow wilder, and as they degenerate into shouting a massenqo takes over the musical improvisation. Then a second soloist joins in.

The second soloist likewise turns to shouting while the massenqo takes up the theme. A third, and even a fourth and succeeding warriors, all take their turn, increasing the decoration of their cries according to their skill.

Exx. 28–30. Extracts of chants in the three 'modes'. Holy Trinity Cathedral, Addis Ababa.

Ex. 28 Ge'ez mode

Rather slow, strongly marked

Ex. 29 'Ezel mode

Slow

Ex. 30 Araray mode

Moderato

Ex. 31. Sixty ecclesiastical chant phrases: source as Exx. 28–30. Each numbered bar represents one notation symbol, or complex of symbols. In fact if all the 60 bars are sung as one continuous chant, phrased at the end of each bar, and with a pause at A, B, C, D and E (after bars 19, 31, 38, 47 and 54), where new sections begin, they represent the chanting of most of the first column of the MS shown in Plate 11. There are obvious close resemblances between certain phrases, or sections of phrases—for example, 29 is 6 expanded to fit a greater number of syllables, and both are represented by the same symbol. The chanting is performed much in the manner of good English psalm-chanting, the words dictating the emphasis in each phrase. Phrases such as 39 have a marked major triad motif; other phrases are strongly pentatonic, especially if two or three are joined together (for example, 6 and 7). Some are far from being pentatonic (see 15 and 58). From the wide variety of phrasal structures found here in only one-third of a page out of a volume of over 200 pages, it is obvious that there is a very considerable number of different phrases, and hence of different notation symbols, in the whole corpus of Ethiopian plain-chant. (See pp. 142-3.)

Ex. 31

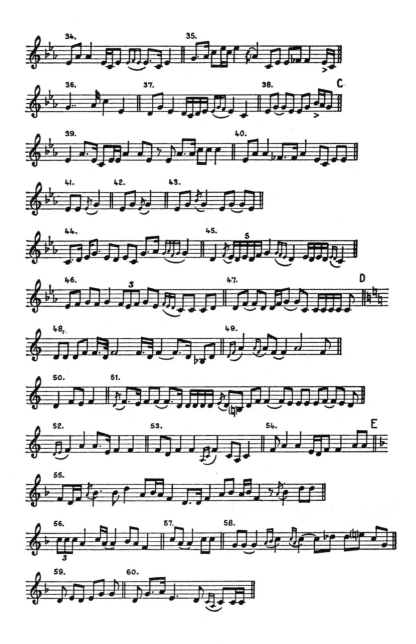

Ex. 32. A hymn chant: quoted by Pankhurst, a transcription from a MS in the Bodleian Library, Oxford.

Ex. 33. Tigre song and dance: Orchestra. The theme is gay, and singing and dancing are combined throughout.

Each phrase is repeated several times. After the last phrase, the song returns to the first two phrases. Drum beats 6 to a bar; washint and massenqo embroider the tune. The chorus repeats whatever the soloist sings.

Ex. 34. Gurage song and dance: Orchestra. From Shoa province. An obvious pentatonic tune, until the irruption of the last solo phrase, which spoils any neat theory of key centre.

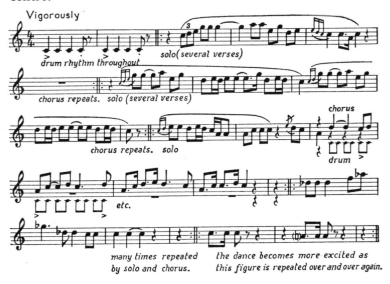

Ex. 35. 'Aychatalehu Yatchaw': Orchestra. An Amhara folk-song. Everyone is dancing and singing happily, except for the soloist, who sees his girl with another lad.

Ex. 36. Dorzai cotton-weaving song: Orchestra. The Dorzai people are a tribe of the Amharas, in Gemu Goffa
province. Their folk-songs are the most distinctive and complex of all Ethiopian music. This is the beginning of a song
in which there are three distinct solo lines and a chorus
melody. As the song develops more singers take up solo
lines, improvising calls like the two-note alternations of the
two men or leaping phrases like the woman's. It grows into
such a thickly-woven web that it is almost impossible to
separate the strands. See Chap. 3 (d) for mention of Dorzai
funeral songs. The overall effect of the tramping rhythm of
the chorus in their songs, with the strongly-syncopated soloists above, is I think the most memorable feature of secular
Ethiopian music, as is the dancing of the priests for ecclesiastical music.

Bibliography

This bibliography lists all the works (marked *) to which reference is made, or from which extracts are quoted, in the text of this book. It also lists some of the works quoted by other writers. It is by no means exhaustive, though I trust it contains all the major sources for musical references, as far as Ethiopia is concerned

I. Major Sources

*Doresse, Jean: *Ethiopia* (trans. Coult), London, 1959; an excellent general survey of the country, and its people and culture.

Grove's Dictionary of Music, especially the articles in Vol. II on the Ethiopian Church and Eastern Church Music.

Lipsky, W.: *Ethiopia—its people and culture*, New York, 1962.

*Mondon-Vidailhet, C.: 'La Musique Ethiopienne' in *Encyclopédie de la Musique et Dictionnaire du Conservatoire*, Paris, 1922; the only study of all aspects of Ethiopian music.

New Oxford History of Music, Vol. II, the articles on early Christian Music, Music of the Eastern Churches, and Ethiopian Music.

*Nettl, Bruno: *Music in Primitive Culture*, Harvard, 1956.

*Pankhurst, Sylvia: *Ethiopia—a cultural history*, London, 1955; the only comprehensive work on every aspect of the country.

*Sachs, Curt: *The Rise of Music in the Ancient World East and West*, New York, 1943.

*Seligman, S.: *Races of Africa*, London, 1939, a simple ethnographic survey.

*Ullendorff, Edward: *The Ethiopians—an introduction to country and people*, 2nd edition, London, 1965; pairs very well with the work by Doresse above.

Wellesz, Egon: 'Studien zur aethiopischen Kirchenmusik' in *Oriens Christianus*, 1920.

BIBLIOGRAPHY

II. Other Sources

Adler, G.: *Handbuch der Musikgeschichte*, 1930.

*Alvares, Fr. Francisco: *The Prester John of the Indies* (trans. Lord Stanley of Adderley, 1881), Cambridge, 1961.

Barblan, G.: *Musiche e strumenti musicale nell 'Africa orientale italiana*, Naples, 1941.

*Baum, James, E.: *Savage Abyssinia*, London, 1928.

Bent, J. Theodore: *The Sacred City of the Ethiopians*, London (?).

*Bose, F. *Musikalische Völkerkunde* (?).

*Bruce: *Travels and Adventure in Ethiopia*, Ed. Clingan, Edinburgh, 1860.

*Budge, Sir E. A. Wallis: *A History of Ethiopia*, London, 1928.

*—: *Legends of Our Lady Mary the Perpetual Virgin and her Mother Hannah*, London, 1933.

*Busk, Douglas: *The Fountains of the Sun*, London, 1957.

*Cheesman, R. E.: *Lake Tana and the Blue Nile*, London, 1936.

Cohen, M.: *Chants éthiopiques*, Paris, 1931.

*Comyn-Platt, Sir Thomas: *The Abyssinian Storm*, London, 1935.

*Fétis: *Historie de la Musique*.

*Gobat, S: *Journal of Three Years' Residence in Abyssinia*, London, 1833.

*Griaule, Marcel: *Abyssinian Journey* (trans. Rich), London, 1935.

*Haberland, Eike et al.: *Altvölker Süd-Äthiopien*, Frankfurt-am-Main, 1959.

Harden, J. M.: *The Anaphora of the Ethiopic Liturgy*, London, 1929.

*Harmsworth, G.: *Abyssinian Adventure*, London, 1935.

Harvard Dictionary of Music, Ed. Willi Apel, London, 1951.

*Hayes, A. J.: *The Source of the Blue Nile*, London, 1905.

Herscher, C.: 'Chants d'Abyssine' in *Zeitschift für Vergleichende Musikwissenschaft II*, 1934.

Hickman, H.: 'Aethiopische Musik' in *Die Musik in Geschichte und Gegenwart*, Kassel, 1949/51.

*Jones, A. M.: *Studies in African Music*, London, 1959.

*Jones, A. H. M. and Monroe, E.: *A History of Ethiopia*, London, 1955.

*Kirby, Percival: *The Musical Instruments of the Native Races of South Africa*, Johannesburg, 1953.

[149]

*Krapf, Ludwig: *Travels*, London, 1860.

*Kyagambiddwa, Joseph: *African Music from the Source of the Nile*, London, 1956.

*Latourette, Kenneth Scott: *A History of Christianity*, London (?).

*Lobo, Fr. Jerome: *A Voyage to Abyssinia* (trans. Legrand), 1735.

Newlandsmith, Ernest: *The Ancient Music of the Coptic Church.*

*Pakenham, Thomas: *The Mountains of Rasselas*, London, 1959.

*Reese, Gustav: *Music in the Middle Ages*, New York, 1940.

*Rey, C. F.: *In the Country of the Blue Nile*, London, 1927.

*—: *The Real Abyssinia*, London, 1935.

*Rossini, C. Cont.: *L'Abissinia*, Rome, 1929.

*Sachs, Curt: *The History of Musical Instruments*, New York, 1940.

Villoteau: *Description de l'Egypte*, Paris, 1799 and 1808.

Zotenburg: *Catalogue des MSS Ethiopiennes de la Bibliothèque Nationale, Paris*, Paris, 1877.

III. Bibliographies

Bibliographies are to be found in many of the above works. Particularly valuable ones are to be found in Budge's *History*, the *New Oxford History of Music*, Nettl's *Music in Primitive Cultures*, and in the following:

*Brandl, Rose: *The Music of Central Africa*. The Hague, 1961.

*Weman, H.: *African Music and the Church in Africa*, Uppsala, 1960.

Glossary

Abyssinian: a word of doubtful etymology; generally refers to any inhabitant of Abyssinia (=Ethiopia); at times loosely used for other peoples of N.E. Africa also.

Aksum: ancient northern Ethiopian city, centre of the great civilization established by Semitic settlers with the Hamitic plateaux peoples.

ambassal: one of the four tuning systems of the krar (q.v.).

Amhara: a northern highlands province of Ethiopia, predominantly Hamitic; the ruling tribe.

Amharic: the language of the Amharas, and the national language of Ethiopia.

anchihoye: one of the four tuning systems of the krar (q.v.).

aquaquam: Ethiopian ecclesiastical dancing.

araray: one of the three moods (often called 'modes') of Ethiopian church chanting.

atamo: small Ethiopian hand-drum.

azmari: Ethiopian troubadour or trouvère.

ba'ati: one of the four tuning systems of the krar (q.v.).

baganna: plucked Ethiopian instrument, usually with ten strings; one of the two forms of Ethiopian lyre (see also krar).

Coptic Church: the Christian (Orthodox) Church of Egypt, based on Alexandria. The name is loosely used to refer to the Ethiopian Christian Church, which also is a Monophysite church.

dawal: Ethiopian bell, usually a sonorous slab of stone or wood.

debtera: a musician or teacher of the Ethiopian Church, on a level with the priesthood, but not an ordained priest.

Dedjazmatch: Ethiopian rank of nobility, taking precedence after Ras (q.v.), and therefore second after the Emperor.

Deggwa: a great collection of hymns for various seasons and ceremonials of the Ethiopian Church's year.

Dorzai: a small Ethiopian Christian tribe of the central plateau, traditionally cotton-weavers, with distinctive tribal music.

ETHIOPIAN MUSIC

embilta: Ethiopian flute, larger and less sophisticated than the washint
(q.v.).
ekphonesis: the cantillation, or quasi-chanting, of the lessons in the
Byzantine liturgy.
Ethiopian: (in this book) Hamitic inhabitant of the central or northern
plateaux, an heir to the true Ethiopian (Hamitic/Semitic) culture.
Ethiopic: Ge'ez (q.v.).
'ezel: one of the three moods (often called 'modes') of Ethiopian
church chanting.
Falasha: strongly Judaic tribe of Ethiopians in the north, called the
Ethiopian Jews.
fukara: warriors' songs, especially from Gojjam (q.v.).
Galla: Hamitic fifteenth- and sixteenth-century invaders of the
Ethiopian plateaux, now widespread throughout the country.
Ge'ez: the language of the Ethiopian Christian Church.
ge'ez: one of the three moods (often called 'modes') of Ethiopian
Church chanting.
Gragne: the Imam Ahmad ibn Ibrahim, nicknamed Gragne, the
Left-Handed, who led the sixteenth-century Muslim conquest of
Ethiopia.
Gojjam: a northern highlands province of Ethiopia, predominantly
Hamitic.
Guragi: a tribe living in the central highlands of Ethiopia.
kabaro: a two-headed Ethiopian kettledrum.
Kebra Negast: 'The Glory of the Kings', a fifteenth-century MS.,
enshrining the saga of Solomon and the Queen of Sheba.
kene: Ethiopian ecclesiastical poetry.
Khedase: the Ethiopian Mass.
kithara: a Greek or Egyptian instrument related to the lyre.
krar: plucked Ethiopian instrument, usually with six strings; one of
the two forms of Ethiopian lyre (see also baganna).
lalibalotch: guild of lepers and their relatives, with particular folk-
music of their own.
leqso: brief, witty or pungent fragment of poetry, usually extem-
porized.
malakat: primitive Ethiopian trumpet.
marawat: Ethiopian handbell.
Maskal: important festival of the Ethiopian Church, celebrating the
finding of the True Cross. The festival comes at the end of the Big
Rains, when the countryside is thick with yellow daisies, the use of

GLOSSARY

which as decorations adds a notable pagan flavour to the ceremony (cf. European Christmas trees, etc.).

massenqo: one-stringed Ethiopian fiddle.

matsahaf: Ethiopian theology and church history.

milikit: the component characters of the Ethiopian church music notation system, consisting of letters and special signs (seraye, q.v.).

mousho: choir, especially at funerals.

mukwamya: prayer-stick carried by a debtera (q.v.), with a thin tang-cross at the top, like a rudimentary crook.

nay: Egyptian flute.

negarit: shallow Ethiopian kettledrum.

qatchel: Ethiopian hand-rattle.

Ras: Ethiopian rank of nobility, taking precedence immediately after the Emperor.

rebab: (= rebec) stringed Arab instrument, like a mandolin but played with a bow.

seraye: interpretation marks added to the milikit (q.v.).

Shankalla: negro or negroid peoples of W. Ethiopia.

Shoa: a central highlands Ethiopian province, predominantly Hamitic.

sistrum: wire hand-rattle used in religious services.

tabot: portable altar, containing the Ark (Commandments).

Tezkar: memorial services held at intervals after a person's death in Ethiopia.

Tigre: a northern highlands province of Ethiopia, predominantly Hamitic.

Timket: Epiphany.

tizita: one of the four tuning systems of the krar (q.v.).

ts'anats'el: Ethiopian sistrum (q.v.).

washint: simple Ethiopian flute.

Yared: a sixth-century saint, variously credited as the originator or codifier of Ethiopian church chanting, and the inventor of the notation system.

zafan: secular Ethiopian song and dance, often improvised.

ziema: Ethiopian liturgical chant.

Index to the Music Examples

Index

warrior songs: *see* fukara

washint (flute): *26–32*, 33, 34, 35, 48–51, 62; Exx. 4, 6, 17, 18, 19, 20, 33; Plates 5, 6

West African music: 127

Wollega province: 19, 46

Wollo province: 27

work songs: 73–4, 76–7

Yared (Saint): 25, 87, 100, *100–5*, 116

zafan (secular song and dance): *72–7*, 83–4

ziema: see liturgical chant

Zour-Amba: 117